At last! A book written for 7 to 14–year olds that tells them what they need to know about the right way to run!

- How running can help kids excel in other sports.
- Why fit students, on the average, do better in school than students who aren't fit.
- What doctors say about children running marathons.
- Why eating just before running isn't a good idea.
- Why runners need to drink plenty of water before, during and after running.
- How to listen to their bodies to avoid injuries.
- What to do about specific aches and pains.
- How to choose the right running shoes and what to wear in all kinds of weather.
- All about warming-up exercises.
- How to start a running program and a running club, and some games to play to make running more fun.

ABOUT THE AUTHORS

Elizabeth G. Barley is a New York City-based writer who has written on health and medical topics for *Good Housekeeping* and *Medical World News*. She is currently working on a non-fiction book.

Mark Bloom, former aerospace correspondent for Reuters and science editor of the New York *Daily News*, is now senior writer at *Medical World News*, McGraw-Hill in New York City. He runs around Central Park reservoir with his dog, Frodo.

YOUNG RUNNERS' HANDBOOK

A GUIDE FOR YOUNG RUNNERS AND THEIR PARENTS

Developed by
Kinney Shoe Corporation

by Elizabeth G. Barley & Mark Bloom

edited by Louise Feinsot

WARNER BOOKS

A Warner Communications Company

WARNER BOOKS EDITION

This Warner Books Edition is published by arrangement with Kinney Shoe Corporation

Designed by Ulrich Ruchti

Black and white photographs, Jonathan Atkin except pages 17, 18, 19, 112, 113.

Cover photo by J. Barry O'Rourke

Warner Books, Inc., 75 Rockefeller Plaza, New York, N.Y. 10019

A Warner Communications Company

Printed in the United States of America

First Printing: June, 1981

10 9 8 7 6 5 4 3 2 1

Contents

Acknowledgments

The YOUNG RUNNERS' HANDBOOK could not have been written without the help and generous support of a great many people – who recognized the *need* for such a book.

We are particularly grateful to Kinney Shoe Corporation for commissioning the book as part of its RUN TO BE FIT public relations program, a program designed to encourage individuals and families to incorporate running and fitness into their lifestyles.

Special thanks go to Kinney executives Cameron I. Anderson, president, John K. Aneser, vice president of marketing communications and Robin Burke, managing director of public relations who remained patient, understanding and supportive while the book was taking shape.

We are grateful to the President's Council on Physical Fitness and Sports for its cooperation and especially to C. Carson Conrad, executive director, for his responsiveness to the completed manuscript and to Glen Swengros, federal state relations, for his assistance to the writers while the book was in progress.

We are indebted to Elizabeth G. Barley, freelance medical writer and editor for her painstaking research and zealous pursuit of accuracy and for sharing with Mark Bloom, senior writer, *Medical World News*, the major responsibility for preparing this work.

The book could not have been completed without the help of Michael Pollock, Ph.D., Director, Department of Medicine, Cardiac Rehabilitation and Center For Evaluation of Human Performance, Mount Sinai Medical Center, Milwaukee, Wisconsin, who graciously consented to review the entire manuscript for accuracy and Clayton Myers, Ph.D., National Director Physical Fitness and Cardiovascular Health, National Council of YMCA's, who prepared the exercise information in Chapter Seven.

Others who gave freely of their time and expertise to help make this project possible include: Angelica Cantlon, M.S.R.D., Nutrition Consultant, American Health Foundation; Dinesh Patel, M.D., Co-director, Sports Medicine Clinic, Massachussets General Hospital; Oded Bar Or, M.D., Director of the Department of Research and Sports Medicine, Wingate Institute, Israel, and Visiting Professor of Pediatrics and Internal Medicine, McMaster University Medical Center, Hamilton, Canada; Elsworth R. Buskirk, Ph.D., Director, Laboratory for Human Performance Research, The Pennsylvania State University; Alan Rogel, M.D., Associate Professor of Orthopedic Surgery, Assistant Professor of Pediatrics and Pharmacology, The Department of Pediatrics, University of Virginia Medical School; Steven Kopits, M.D., Associate Professor of Orthopedic Surgery, Assistant Professor of Pediatrics, The Johns Hopkins Hospital; David Brody, M.D., Chief of Surgical Specialities, Group Health Associations, Inc.; G. Lawrence Rarick, Ph.D., Department of Physical Education, University of California, Berkeley; Martin Gruber, M.D., Assistant Professor of Orthopedics, State University of Stony Brook, School of Medicine, New York; Fred W. Kasch, Ph.D., Professor and Exercise Laboratory Director, San Diego State University; Elizabeth Coryllos, M.D., Chief of Pediatric Surgery, Mercy Hospital, Rockville Centre, New York; Kurt Hirschorn, M.D., Chairman of Department of Pediatrics, Mount Sinai Hospital, New York and Oliver Grant, Head Coach CYO Track Club, Head Coach Cross Country Running, St. Alban's School, Washington, D.C.

Robert Bagar, creative director of Ruder & Finn, Inc. (and an avid runner), was responsible for first directing Kinney's attention to the merits of a comprehensive running program for young people. The idea for a book directed to young runners was conceived and its editorial approach worked out by Louise Feinsot, vice president at Ruder & Finn, Inc., who acted as overall editor of the work.

Others who played a vital role in the production of the book include: Ulrich Ruchti of Ruder & Finn Design, the book's designer who created the exciting graphic-design elements; Jessica Miller, copy editor and photo researcher; Richard Timperio, illustrator; Jonathan Atkin, whose excellent black and white photographs enhance each chapter of the book and J. Barry O'Rourke whose superb color photograph appears on the cover.

Finally, we want to thank all the many kind people (too numerous to list) who directed the writers and editors of this book to new sources of information and who answered frequent queries on the telephone during the many months that it took to prepare this work

Preface

Children are God's and man's most precious possession. We parents prize them highly and are very concerned for their welfare. Fitness is a critical aspect of a child's development. However, we often forget that children need four to six hours of vigorous physical activity each day for total physical and mental well-being.

A recent national survey has shown that American children have not improved their physical fitness over the past ten years. It is clear that with so many things vying for children's time, there is a need to have exercise programmed into their daily lives. The introduction of a running program in our schools as a way to help build our children's total fitness may be the answer — even for the most budget-poor of our elementary and secondary schools.

Running does not rely on expensive equipment nor does the class size have to be restricted to maintain an appropriate student to instructor or student to equipment ratio. By contrast, with sports such as tennis, racquetball or basketball, the number of courts limits usage and class size, adding to the cost of instruction. This does not mean that recreational and sport instruction should be eliminated but rather that it can be partially replaced by this kind of a much needed aerobic activity.

Young people should be encouraged to incorporate an aerobic exercise regimen into their lifestyles. Research findings have shown that atherosclerosis, one of the primary causes of ischemic heart disease (IHD) — the leading cause of death in America today — often begins during childhood. Since vigorous exercise appears to have an effect on several risk factors associated with IHD and is associated with a decreased risk in developing IHD, it is important that children begin to develop good exercise habits at an early age. Also, few would question the positive effect that vigorous exercise has on the quality of life.

Most adults are now aware of the need for regular exercise. They have been alerted to the detrimental effects of an inactive existence through the innumerable books that have been written for them on fitness and running in the past few years. But there are no equivalent books on the subject for children. *Young Runners' Handbook, A Guide for Young Runners and Their Parents*, therefore, is a most welcome addition to the fitness/running literature.

This book, which was written especially for children ages seven to fourteen, offers young people the necessary guidance for embarking on a safe, fitness-building running program. I congratulate the authors and editors of this painstakingly researched book for preparing a much needed document which no doubt will have an important long-range impact on the health and well-being of children and future adults of America.

Fred W. Kasch, Ph.D.
Professor and Exercise Laboratory Director
San Diego State University
San Diego, California

Michael L. Pollock, Ph.D.
Department of Medicine
Director
Cardiac Rehabilitation and Center
For Evaluation of Human Performance
Mount Sinai Medical Center
Milwaukee, Wisconsin

Letter from Cameron I. Anderson

There is an important reason for this book: how young Americans can achieve healthier, more satisfying lives by improving their performance in the activity most spontaneous and natural to them from early childhood, *vigorous running*. Ever notice how young tots spring to life — and forever run to get where they're going? Running can be equated with enthusiasm in the world of the young.

Many new books have been written over the past three years to pique an interest in running. Yet the special needs of young runners have been seriously overlooked.

We believe the timely remedy is at hand between the covers of this comprehensive volume, representing the collective knowledge of running authorities, along with prominent medical and physical education specialists in fitness training.

Discover running at an early age, point out our authors, and the rewards and satisfactions can be immense and of lifelong benefit to the individual. Start running to get more out of life, for self-esteem and self-discovery, running for joy — and running for the sheer health of it. Maximum advantages accrue, it is clear, from entry into the runner's world early in the life cycle.

Running's a journey of discovery, a journey without end. It is the hope of the book's authors and sponsors that the reading process will prove to be but a prelude to the real business at hand — participation in the active life for decades hence; and a beginning, for more Americans, of a heightened state of existence in this lovely land of ours.

To put these reflections about the future in a national resource perspective, it is vital for America that each young person strives to reach his or her potential. Demographics of the 80's and 90's indicate there will be fewer children as our national birthrate continues to decline. In the face of such a reality, society must be encouraged to shun the sedentary life before the lack of vigor atrophies the ability of our citizenry to cope with the strict demands and exigencies of the times.

There are clear opportunities for parents, educators, governmental agencies and, of course, young Americans themselves, to utilize the information in this book to design a practical running regimen adjusted to the chronological requirements and individual make-up of participants.

However, the *push* should not come from without. The push, for maximum effect, should come from individual understanding of just what it takes and what is at stake. Hence a faithful reading of YOUNG RUNNERS' HANDBOOK, A Guide for Young Runners and Their Parents, is recommended.

I congratulate the authors, editors and contributors of this carefully researched book for preparing a document which will doubtless inspire many to build a significant new component of physical fitness into their lives. All Americans will be the beneficiaries.

Cameron I. Anderson
President
Kinney Shoe Corporation

Why Run?

1

We're going to tell you about running and how to have a good time doing it. This isn't a book about how nice it is to run. That's for you to find out if you haven't already. We're going to give you an idea of how to run, how to do it well and how to make your body work for you.

But why run? For those of you who are wearing out your second or third pair of running shoes, maybe that's not much of a question. You've got your own answers — and they're all good ones, whatever they are. But for those of you just starting, or thinking about starting, here's one reason you might want to make a habit of running: it'll help to make you fit.

It's true not too many of you are actually unfit. At least not unfit in the fat-and-forty sense. But a lot of you may be closer to it than you think. This is because there's a lot more to fitness than looking like you're in shape.

You can be way out of shape even if you look lean and hard. You can't see blood pressure or cholesterol, but you could have higher levels of one or both than is good for you. Many children do. And, if you're overweight, you're probably all too well aware of it.

All these things add to the chance that when you're forty, you may be one of the out-of-shape variety of adults.

Right now a lot of you are at the point where you're ready to begin a lifelong decline in physical fitness. Just a few years ago, physiologists were saying that the average American woman peaked in physical fitness when she was only ten or twelve years old. Imagine, being over the hill at ten or twelve. For men the picture wasn't much better. Their lifelong fitness decline began at eighteen to twenty-two — not until then because they were more active in high school and college.

But something's happening. Take a look outside and you'll see that millions of Americans are making up for the youthful folly of letting themselves get unfit. They are running. We are in the first peacetime fitness boom in America's history. It's also the first time that women in great numbers have joined in with enthusiasm in exercise.

Your advantage

There's only one good way to keep yourself from ever getting out of shape: stay in it. It's easier for you now but remember that if you don't take steps to stay fit, it won't be too long before you aren't. Then it gets hard.

Now you may wonder why we're talking so much about running and fitness. Aren't there other things you can do to stay fit? Why not soccer, or swimming, or tennis? All good questions and if you keep reading you'll find out

that running is just one road to fitness, and it can build you up for other sports.

If you aren't interested in running, keep reading anyway. You may find out why. Moreover, as Kermit the Frog once noted sagely, "You never know when a $5 bill is going to fall out of a book."

Kermit's got the right idea. Life is full of surprises.

What's in store?

We're going to cover a whole lot of ground about fitness generally and about running that we think you'll find pretty interesting. We may not rivet you to the chair, and you may even find it's possible to put this book down once or twice before finishing it. But if you're a runner or a potential runner, you may find it a good reference when things happen to your body you don't quite understand.

You'll discover there's a difference between the running you do for soccer or football and the running you do for distance (in a nutshell, it's that distance running can give you stamina for the other sports). We'll tell you whether a cheeseburger or a taco, or both, just before running gives you the fuel you need for extra miles. (Don't believe it.) We'll go into how your body is an efficient machine and what it takes to keep it humming along smoothly. And, if you read closely, you'll find out why you keep getting taller and your mother and father don't.

And there's more

Keep tuned in and you'll discover fascinating tidbits about how running actually improves the ability of a heart to pump blood (though at your age, it does a pretty good job even if you don't lace up a pair of running shoes).

You'll learn whether running helps you lose weight (if you want to); what it means if you're running and something hurts; what to do on a hot day; how much water to drink and when to drink it; how to start running; how to stretch your muscles to keep from straining anything; how to enter competitions if you're good at running; and, finally, how much damage your feet are doing to the earth with all this running (just a little joke to see if you're still with us).

Some facts to confuse you

Okay. Ready to run? Not yet, huh? Well, we've got a couple of more points before you get to the juicy stuff.

• President Carter loves to jog. Ex-President Ford, once a football player for the University of Michigan and always a swimmer, is also very fit. Carter beat Ford, proving that no matter how fit you are, you can both win and lose a Presidential election.

• Study after study has shown that fit students, on the average, do better in school than students who aren't fit, and that getting fit tends to help raise your grades—maybe because you are more alert in class or can stay awake longer to do homework. It isn't clear why it hap-

Grete Waitz winning the 1979 "L'eggs Mini Marathon."

pens. But it does. To be sure, out-of-shape people often do very well in school and later in life. It's just that they are working at a disadvantage.

• Jogging won't win you the Nobel Prize. That takes genius. But if you're lucky enough to be a genius, fitness may give you the stamina and drive to fulfill your brilliant potential.

• Several thousand doctors are members of the American Medical Joggers Association. Most of them will tell you they run for pure enjoyment and to keep their weight down. Ask them if fitness is the road to a long life, they'll tell you nobody knows for sure—but they aren't taking any chances.

• Chris Evert Lloyd jogs every day to sustain her endurance for those three-set struggles against Martina Navratilova, who, naturally, jogs every day to keep herself in trim for three sets against Chris. No way could Muham-

Distance running gives you stamina for other sports.

Photo Photo Researchers Inc./Harvey Barad

mad Ali have gone fifteen rounds—or even five rounds—if he hadn't done his daily roadwork.

A side trip to space

The nation's astronauts were jogging back in the days when it was still looked on by most people as something only a "health nut" would do. One of them, Alan Bean, sorely missed that daily run when he was in orbit for two months aboard Skylab.

Bean had suffered from a back problem in the Navy, long before NASA borrowed him for space duty. But his exercise and fitness program built up a thick layer of back muscles to support his spine and his back pain disap-

Running plays an important part in many other sports.

Photo Photo Researchers Inc./Michael Philip Manheim

peared. He jogged daily and did other exercises to keep fit.

But in orbit, there is no gravity. An astronaut is weightless inside his spacecraft; he floats from place to place effortlessly. It's very unlike earth, where even sitting on a chair or standing still requires muscular effort because of gravity. NASA doctors, not to mention Bean and his two crewmates, had long been aware that in a spaceship, the lack of exercise makes muscles and bones slowly lose their strength. It doesn't matter in space — where strength isn't needed. But what happens on return to earth?

Well, in the long Skylab flights the astronauts tried as hard as they could to exercise, using stationary bicycles. But poor Bean. That thick layer of muscle supporting his spine just faded away with only two months of inactivity, and he was in agony when he returned to earth. It took him about two years to build himself up again.

Supply and demand

Nature has given our bodies an almost unlimited capacity to adjust to physical work. Everything in this book is based on that principle, your body's ability to adjust to demand. The more you run, the more your body will respond and the better shape you'll be in.

The reverse is also true. Just as nature responds to increased demands, it also reacts to decreased activity. That's why you have to continue to exercise to maintain fitness or to develop it in the first place. Say, for example, that a moose kicks you, you break your leg badly and have to stay in bed for weeks with the leg in traction. Finally, you're allowed up on crutches. What's happened? The leg muscle is weaker and smaller and the bone is weaker because it has lost calcium. No different from Alan Bean and his experience with weightlessness in orbit.

There's just no way to store fitness. If you don't use it, you lose it.

Running is one way to keep yourself in good condition. Athletes use it all the time. When coaches make their players run, they're building up the endurance that is needed for these sports. In short, the fit running back gets to the hole in the line as fast in the last quarter as he does in the first. The young gymnast needs endurance to be as sharp in her floor exercises as she was on the uneven parallel bars. Cathy Rigby, needless to say, jogs to stay in condition.

So what's it all about?

These people, whether astronauts, athletes or Presidents, who are taking to jogging are doing it for several reasons.

- It takes only a few months to build stamina or general conditioning with a running program. One half hour three times a week should do it.

- It's cheap. Basically, all you need is a good pair of running shoes.

- It can be done almost anywhere, anytime.

- It takes very little skill—unless you get serious.

- It builds confidence. Almost every runner reports new feelings of self-esteem.

- With the gasoline shortage, you may need it to get from place to place. As one of Finland's top marathoners, Esa Tikkanen, commented on why his country turned out so many leading distance runners, "Back home it costs $2.40 a gallon for gas."

Running makes you feel good. It's clearly your own thing—no balls, no bats, no rackets. You can run when you want to, at the pace you choose and cover as much or as little distance as your heart desires.

You make the rules when you run. Feel the wind or the rain in your face. Run one mile or ten. Hang loose. Shuffle. Skip along.

Have fun.

The Fitness Game

2

Take a look at the bushels of gold medals U. S. athletes haul home from the Olympics every four years, and it seems like American kids must be about as fit as they can possibly be. But it just isn't so, and don't fool yourselves. Decathlon champ Bruce Jenner wasn't an average American kid. You are.

Once again, there may not be too many of you who are unfit *yet* — not as unfit as a lot of adults in this country. But the average American your age probably can't do a lot of things that the run-of-the-mill Swedish or Japanese kid can do. Scandinavians of all ages are out there pushing the pedals of bicycles every day, and most Japanese students are well-trained in judo.

A national fitness survey, done some years ago, showed that the only fitness test Americans your age excelled at was throwing a softball. (And it's not even considered a fitness test any more.) That upset a lot of people in this country. But what really riled them was when British *girls,* age ten to thirteen, beat American *boys* the same age in just about everything.

We were eating better and living better. But they were fitter. They could climb ropes better, do more push-ups and chin-ups and run farther and faster. All we could do was toss a softball. Something was definitely wrong.

These 1957 tests of the fitness of American youth were dismaying. We were soft. Too much sitting in front of the TV or not enough gym classes in school? Nobody knew why. But a lot of people were worried. And a lot of people are still worried.

So, new physical education programs were started in the schools. The White House got involved and fitness became a national priority.

The national fitness survey was tried again in 1965. There were significant improvements for both boys and girls. It was very encouraging. Fitness levels were still not where experts felt they should be, but the national muscle was firming up.

Then came 1975 and the national testing program was carried out again. There was only a little good news this time. Girls generally did better in the flexed arm hang, standing long jump and the endurance run, which were three of the seven testing events.

But boys showed no significant improvement over the scores from ten years earlier. Fourteen-year-old boys actually scored worse in the standing long jump. One out of every six boys couldn't do a simple chin-up. One out of every thirty-six couldn't do even fifteen sit-ups.

What American youth seemed to lack most was endurance and upper body strength. And, just as this was being learned, one of the most important ways to get you fit was having troubles—school physical education programs. In many schools, everything had gotten so expensive that fitness programs had to be cut back or cut out.

Youth to the rescue

Well, just as it looked like we were in danger of breeding a generation of marshmallows, something happened. You discovered your legs. No longer would you just stand around in an outfield waiting for someone to hit you with a fly ball. You found soccer. And ice hockey. Some of you even took to the tennis courts or the hiking trails.

Around the same time a lot of people, including kids, started running just for enjoyment. More and more of you are doing it. And some people hope it may be paying off. If you develop a habit of running now, when young, chances are you can keep it all your life. And that means fitness may be yours for a lifetime. Running won't do it all, of course. You'll have to be sure you always do exercises that tone the rest of your body, too. Not just your legs—and heart.

Many schools still aren't suggesting in gym classes that you run, and you may have to do it on your own. This may change: there's some talk of more schools incorporating running as part of their physical education programs. After all, it solves many money problems because it requires no expensive equipment.

But most gym classes still emphasize games — softball, basketball, field hockey or touch football. There isn't much offered in the way of distance running or swimming.

Two kinds of conditioning

Distance running and swimming are what we mean when we talk about *aerobic* exercise. Very simply, aerobic exercise is what gets your heart in shape for the sports you're going to play.

Actually, it's a little more complicated than that. Any continuous, rhythmical exercise , such as running, biking, swimming, cross-country skiing and enthusiastic walking, that uses large muscle groups is aerobic. *Anerobic* exercise is characterized by short bursts of explosive activity.

The steady jog — aerobic exercise. The sprint — anerobic exercise.

Its pure form is sprinting, but it's part of many other sports — tennis, football and soccer, to name a few. Depending on how intensely they're played, such sports offer a combination of these two types of conditioning. That's why boys and girls who stay active in sports in high school and college don't begin their decline in fitness until later than those who don't.

Both types are important to all-round fitness. Aerobic exercise builds general stamina or endurance — what's called general conditioning. Anerobic exercise builds endurance in specific muscles, depending on the sport or activity.

In truth, a *total* fitness program has many elements — and is hard to come by. To get the most fit professional team in the NFL, Dallas Cowboy coach Tom Landry has his players do distance running for general conditioning, sprinting for anerobic conditioning, weight lifting for strength, and some yoga-type exercises for flexibility. (That's why we've added the strengthening and stretching exercises to your running warm-ups in Chapter Seven.)

The importance of general conditioning or endurance training is this: if you want to get in shape for one set of tennis, just play tennis. But if you want to get in shape for three sets of tennis, and be as fresh playing the third set as you were playing the first, a running program will help you do it. Running increases your aerobic capacity and this means your cardiovascular system is tuned up.

You've gotta have heart

That's what endurance training is all about. Cardiovascular fitness, circulatory fitness, aerobic power. They all mean the same thing. They mean your heart is strong enough to pump the blood you need for all this exercise. And your muscles have the capability of using it.

By now all of you have heard about your heart. It's the muscle that pumps blood to the rest of your body. But most of us have only a hazy understanding of why that's important. About all most people really know is that it involves breathing and oxygen. Actually, what happens is fascinating.

Your heart works day and night, squeezing and opening

about seventy-two times a minute when you're just sitting around. Actually that's average for an adult. Yours beats faster depending upon how young you are: if you're twelve, it's about seventy-nine times a minute. Your heart beats still faster when you're walking quickly, or when you're angry or upset. It may beat as fast as 200 times a minute when you've been running at full tilt for awhile. When you're asleep, your heart gets its rest, too. It slows down to about forty-five or fifty beats a minute.

Taking your pulse

Put your hand to your chest, and you can time your heart. Use a watch with a second hand. Just count the beats for fifteen seconds, and multiply by four. Presto, you've got it. Or, if you want, count the beats for thirty seconds and multiply by two. It's your choice.

Another way to time your heart is to take your own pulse, just like you've seen doctors do. Put your fingers on your wrist—you'll feel the pulse after a little practice—and time the pulse just as if your hand were on your chest. When you take your pulse, you feel your blood reacting to the beat of your heart—a little spurt every time your heart beats.

The reason you touch your wrist—instead of your nose—for your pulse is that there is a blood vessel running between your arm and hand that is convenient to reach and easy to feel. Actually, there are many places on your body where you could take your pulse. You probably can find some of them easily.

The big beat

Your heart beats about 100,000 times a day or more, sending your blood on more than 4,000 daily trips through miles and miles of blood vessels. Incredibly, those daily trips mean your heart circulates some 4,000 gallons of blood over twenty-four hours.

That's a lot of work. The goal of endurance training is to make your heart do more with less effort. When you're fit, your heart pumps the same amount of blood with fewer beats per minute — about sixty compared with the average adult's seventy-two. Many runners have hearts that beat only forty to fifty times a minute when they are just standing around. That means that a fit person's heart may beat 17,280 times fewer a day than someone who's out of shape. Over a lifetime, that adds up.

A deep breath

Obviously, your blood would wear out pretty quickly with all those trips around the body if something wasn't done about it. Well, one thing that's done is that you breathe a lot, about ten to fourteen breaths a minute if you're just sitting around. That gets oxygen into you, which is the whole point of your blood's circulation.

Oxygen keeps us going. As your blood circulates, it goes to all the body's parts, feeding the billions of individual cells that, collectively, make up you. Blood takes oxygen to these cells. We get energy from the food we eat, but we need oxygen to carry out the transformation of food to energy. This process is happening all the time in all our cells.

Some cells need more oxygen than others. Brain cells need a constant supply of oxygen. Cut the brain off from oxygen for four minutes, give or take a few seconds, and the brain dies—and so do you. That's what happens when someone drowns. Your body stores energy in the form of food, but you can't store oxygen. Try holding your breath. Your body needs oxygen so desperately that you just can't do it for more than a minute, or maybe a little over that.

Luckily oxygen is available (and free) in the air. With every breath you take, fresh oxygen enters your lungs. There, the oxygen attaches to red blood cells, and the blood flows to the heart which sends the oxygen-rich blood to the waiting body. It streams out via arteries—like the one you can feel pulsing in your wrist—and to individual cells via smaller vessels called capillaries.

The cells draw oxygen and other chemicals from the blood. At the same time the cells throw out waste in the form of carbon dioxide. The blood returns to the heart and lungs via capillaries first and then larger vessels called veins.

Back in the lungs, the exchange is reversed. The waste carbon dioxide is given to the lungs, and the blood takes on a fresh supply of oxygen for another trip. You get rid of the carbon dioxide when you exhale and you take in fresh oxygen when you inhale. And so it goes, huff and puff.

Big-hearted kids

Actually, it wasn't so long ago that doctors thought that people your age couldn't handle really strenuous exercise like distance running. They thought your hearts weren't strong enough—that your hearts couldn't pump the extra blood that hard exercise requires. But then in 1937, doctors found out that the 19th-century scientist who issued the warning had been wrong. He had used the wrong formula, and no one had ever double-checked him. It was as simple as that.

In fact, many people believe that the ten-year-old is the best-suited person of all for exercise, pound for pound. That doesn't mean you ten-year-olds should be setting world records. It means your heart and muscles, compared with your body fat and general size, make you more efficient human machines now than you will ever be again.

Ten-year-olds don't beat Bill Rodgers or Frank Shorter in marathons, but only because the big guys have longer legs and stronger muscles. Besides, most ten-year-olds are far too busy enjoying themselves to run marathons. As far as we're concerned, a couple of miles a few times a week is just fine. Really, it doesn't matter how *far* you run: thirty minutes three to five times a week is enough. The idea is to enjoy running.

Right now, even if the best you can do is run to the dinner

table, most of you have a more efficient heart than adults who don't exercise regularly. But you'll be an adult before you know it.

Fitness fits in

How does all this fit in with running and fitness? The frequent runner's heart grows stronger and more efficient. So do his respiratory muscles and leg muscles.

• The heart of the average unfit person sends about two ounces of blood into circulation for every beat. An enthusiastic week-end marathoner like Dr. George Sheehan has a heart that gives his body five ounces of blood per heart beat. And world-class marathoners sometimes have hearts that eject eight ounces of blood per beat—four times as much as the unfit person.

• At the same time, runing makes the diaphragm—the muscle that helps you breathe—stronger so you can move oxygen in and out at a faster rate. The body's cells use the oxygen they get at a faster rate and the carbon dioxide waste is removed more efficiently from the cells.

• Any regular exercise increases the ability of muscles to accept oxygen from the blood, helping to keep you from getting tired.

• What's more, distance running can make your muscles more efficient; reactions happen more quickly and effectively. This is because your muscles can store more energy in the form of glycogen (see Chapter Four) and the number of mitochondria (think of them as the muscle's power pack) increase.

• There is an ongoing debate among physicians as to what role running and aerobic fitness play in the prevention of heart attacks that affect so many of the older generation, a generation that will someday be you. But there is virtually no disagreement among doctors about one thing: the style of living practiced by most runners is good for their hearts.

Most runners aren't overweight. Most runners don't smoke. Some runners eat foods that are low in cholesterol and saturated fats. And though there are exceptions, people whose weight is down, who don't smoke and whose cholesterol is low have less trouble with heart disease.

See your doctor

Most of you will have no trouble moving into distance running. But some of you have conditions that need a doctor's advice on how to go about starting an endurance program. It may help if you can find a doctor who's a runner, because he will have personal experience with some of the pitfalls and problems. If you have one of the following conditions (or even if you don't) and would like to find a doctor in your area, write: The American Academy of Pediatrics, P.O. Box 1034, Evanston, Illinois 60024, Attn: Committee on Physical Fitness, Recreation and Sports, for their recommendation.

DIABETES: Since insulin dosage is critical, it's best for juvenile diabetics to check with their doctors before starting a distance running program. Regular exercise can (though not always) change your insulin requirements: many diabetics have been able to reduce their dosage when running regularly.

RHEUMATIC HEART: Young people with rheumatic heart disease should see their doctor before starting a running program. He will be able to give you the appropriate test to see if your heart is up to the exercise. Most are. It helps, as always, to ease into the program and let your heart get used to the extra demand that's going to be placed on it.

ASTHMA: Most asthmatic children can handle a running program. Find a physician knowledgeable about the effects of exercise on asthma. He may recommend that you precede exercise with a warm-up period. Besides stretching tight muscles, warm-ups prior to exercise may reduce the amount of asthma resulting from the exercise. If you require medication daily to keep your asthma under control, then one of the first recommendations will be that you *not forget* to take the medicine properly. If you require "extra" medication to keep the endurance exercise from triggering asthma, the timing is usually crucial. Pay close attention to your doctor's instructions.

Remember that Teddy Roosevelt, one of our most vigorous Presidents, was a frail asthmatic as a youth, but he built himself up through a variety of outdoor sports. "Bully," as Teddy liked to say.

Start now

Nobody knows how much running it takes to get your cardiovascular system in condition. It varies from person to person. But here's how a little effort can improve matters.

Some junior high school boys in Texas with no special running training averaged 1.2 miles for the 12-minute run. In gym class they started jogging five minutes a day, gradually increasing it over fifteen weeks to fourteen minutes a day. Then they were tested again for the 12-minute run, and they averaged 1.5 miles—a 17.5% increase.

In California, girls eight to thirteen were given a special twelve-week training course, running up to seven minutes four or five times a week. Their aerobic power was up 18% after six weeks, and it was up 26% after twelve weeks.

There are all sorts of complicated ways to tell whether you are improving in your running, but the easiest way is to just think back a couple of months. Was that three miles real tough then, and is it pretty easy now? Can you finish now in a sprint? Are you doing that extra few miles without having to talk yourself into it? Remember, the only way to improve your aerobic power is to gradually do more—either a little faster or a little farther, or both.

And most important: are you looking forward to running?

Twelve-week Mileage Chart

WEEKS		
EXAMPLE		
1ST		
2ND		
3RD		
4TH		
5TH		
6TH		
7TH		
8TH		
9TH		
10TH		
11TH		
12TH		
MILES 0	½	1

Start keeping a record of how far you run each day. Can you reach two-and-one-half miles after twelve weeks?

1½ 2 2½

Growing Up

3

Jog a couple of steps. Seems simple enough. But just to take those few steps, your body does some dazzling feats. That's a very capable body you've got working for you. Here's a hint of what's going on as you take those few steps:

- More than 150 bones are working to propel you.

- Dozens of muscles are fighting against gravity to move those bones.

- Tendons and ligaments and cartilage are working to keep muscles and joints and bones working in tandem.

It's all known as your musculoskeletal system. And it's designed to move you from place to place, at a rate you choose. Running is a natural pace but it can stress this system and runners are always worried about bits and pieces of it breaking down (see Chapter Five).

There are sixty-two bones in your hips, legs and feet that are moving smoothly to carry you forward. In your feet alone, there are twenty muscles that are in action for those couple of steps.

As you pump your arms, sixty-four bones in your hands, arms, and shoulders are acting to give you momentum.

There are twenty-six more bones in your spine that give shape and structure to your body. As you jog those few steps, many of the eighty-odd movable joints in your body are helping to keep the bones moving smoothly.

It starts with the brain sending a message along your nervous system to all those muscles. The message reads: run. So the muscles contract and pull on the tendons, the tendons move the bones, and you're off and running.

Whether you're eight or seventy-eight, that's how your musculoskeletal system moves you along. The big difference is that you're still growing up. And that matters when you run.

Skeletons that grow

For one thing, you have what doctors call an "immature"

musculoskeletal system. This means, basically, that your skeleton hasn't grown to its full height yet, and you have only about half the muscle strength, in proportion to your body, that you will have a few years from now.

Besides, growth is a much more complex process than just getting taller and stronger. Bodies (human ones, at least) aren't completely developed until age twenty or twenty-one. That's when you physically become an adult, literally *a grown-up*. Maybe that's why the traditional age of manhood and womanhood is twenty-one.

Mind you, how old you are doesn't indicate exactly how much you've developed — it's more like a ballpark figure. If, for instance, you're a twelve-year-old girl who doesn't yet have breasts and your girlfriends do, take heart. Each person develops in her or his own way and time, according to a genetic blueprint (of which you'll hear more about in a bit.)

But, no matter how far along the way you are, you still aren't grown up yet. Right now you're preparing for, beginning, or into the second very rapid growing period of your life. The first was when you changed from an infant to a walking, talking, demanding two-year-old.

If you're younger than ten or eleven, some of you are taking on extra fat to be used as a source of energy during this "adolescent growth spurt." If you're older, an increase in sex hormones may already be starting to change and shape your body. And, most likely, your nervous system is more excitable than an adult's. You cry more easily than most grown-ups, don't you? You probably laugh more, too.

All of this matters. What a lot of doctors think is that the whole process of growth (which nobody understands completely) makes children more susceptible to even everyday stresses and strains. No wonder they worry about the effect of strenuous exercise.

How far is up?

But let's look specifically at your legs. One of the first

things that happens during this growth spurt is that you reach your full height. One of the reasons, by the way, that boys generally are taller and bigger in their late teens and for the rest of their lives is that they get about a year more to grow during this period. Sex hormones make a difference though, too.

Naturally, the bones that are responsible for you getting taller are the long bones of your legs. If you're not getting tall as fast as you want, don't try to hang from trees by your arms. It won't work. You can't pull yourself up by your shoulders.

At the joints at the ends of these long leg bones are growth plates. Your maximum height depends on these growth plates. And that was decided before you were born. The genetic blueprint you inherited from your parents is in your cells. When your genes calculate you've reached your destined altitude, your growth plates will stop expanding.

Nobody has ever figured a way to make people grow taller, except to improve nutrition. Poor nutrition, among other things, can cut inches (or centimeters, if you've gone metric). Good nutrition can't make you grow taller than your genes intend, but it'll help to make sure you'll get there.

Kareem Abdul-Jabbar of the Los Angeles Lakers would have been very tall even if he'd eaten poorly as a kid—though maybe not quite the seven-footer that he is. And shortstop Freddy Patek of the Kansas City Royals ate very well as a kid, but five feet, six inches was all nature had in store for him.

American-style diets in Japan after World War II significantly increased the height of Japanese children. In this country, generation after generation of kids are taller than their parents because of improved nutrition. But the latest figures from the government say that, in general, we've reached our genetic growth destiny. In other words, Americans of tomorrow—you—will be no taller than Americans of today.

As Abe Lincoln replied when asked how long a person's legs should be, "Just long enough to reach the ground."

Go, plates, grow

As long as these growth plates (called epiphyses) at your leg joints remain soft, your leg bones will keep growing. When you are growing, the ends of your long bones are cartilage that hardens into bone. As this happens new cartilage keeps forming. And as the new cartilage keeps forming—at these growth plates—you keep growing. But that day will come...

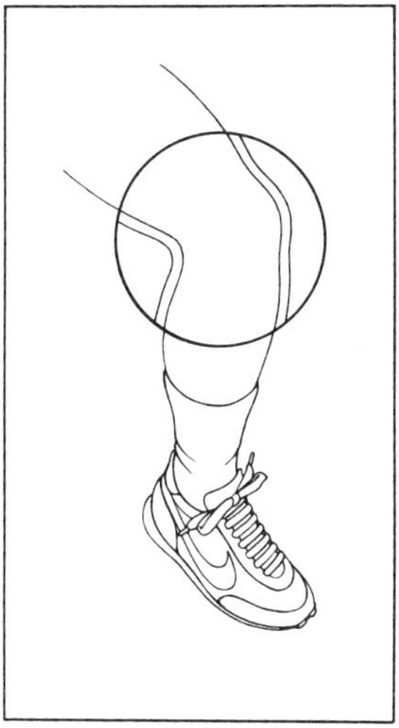
Growth plates at the knee.

If you looked inside the hip joints of your parents, for instance, you would find that these growth plates had hardened. That's why your parents stopped growing. And that's why you, too, will stop growing some day. The cartilage stops forming, the bones harden once and for all and that's your ultimate altitude.

How far to run?

Now, back to running. Some doctors are worried that too much stress (all that pavement pounding) will injure these soft, still-expanding growth plates. When that happens (as it has, for instance, in accidents that are completely unrelated to exercise), growth can be stunted. But not to worry. So far—and more and more kids have been running in the past few years—doctors report no increase in injuries to these growth plates.

The problem is that nobody knows how much exercise is too much exercise. It's difficult to study its effect on people because there are so many other factors that contribute to wellbeing — what they eat, how they live, do they take care of themselves? And even if we knew how much and what kind of exercise is best for what person, there would still be questions about how running affects a developing body. Very few studies have been done on children, more on boys than on girls.

Still, what most doctors say (and it's their job to be cautious) is that running is a child's natural activity. What might not be good is running twenty-six miles in a marathon. That could be too much stress on the growth plates, particularly at the knee. Even this advice is qualified though. If you find you love running and want to take on that challenge (remember that twenty-six miles is just an arbitrary figure; it's not magic and some doctors think the distance is too long even for adults), you'll have to be serious enough about it to train with a good coach and be under the care of a good orthopedist.

The other way you could injure your growth plates is to stumble and fall (see Chapter Five). Since about the age of five, you've had good control of the muscles involved in running, and eye-foot coordination develops by age seven or so. Technically, you're all set to run smoothly but, like anything else, some people are more skilled than others. Also, when you're growing this rapidly, your body is naturally more awkward. Teenage boys who play football and other sports with a lot of body contact, often get hurt more easily, particularly at the joints. That spurt — when your body's in such a state of flux — makes you more vulnerable to injuries.

Toward incredible hulk

Now, about your muscles. They're what move you. When people talk about "lazy bones" they really mean lazy muscles. One of the ways of making sure you get stronger is to use those muscles. They don't start strong, you know. They have to be worked into shape, and that isn't easy if you've ignored them for a long time. One nice thing is that your muscles take three times longer to grow weak than they do to get strong.

Muscles can only do so much. For a runner, the ideal combination is strong leg muscles and a thin body. And it generally works out that, as you run to get fit, your leg muscles get stronger and your body gets thinner. Then, with less fat to carry, your muscles can do more. And, as you do more, your muscles get still more powerful.

As we told you earlier, ten-year-olds are very efficient running machines but they don't set world records. You won't have powerful enough muscles to do that until you grow up. So, even though you may have better aerobic power now (see Chapter Two) than you will in a few years, you'll be a faster, stronger runner then – if you keep running.

Moving your way

Your musculoskeletal system does more than just move you along. It helps protect all your internal organs. And inside your bones is a substance called bone marrow, where new red blood cells are being made all the time. Bones store two important minerals, calcium and phosphorus. And they give you shape, some form and structure. Your skeleton really supports the rest of your body.

So treat it well. Listen and watch for signs of strain. Don't stress it by running too long or too far. Don't be pushed farther than you want. Running isn't work. It should be fun—most of the time, at least.

Some high school kids today hate running. Why? Because, once upon a time, running laps used to be punishment. Other kids have resented the all-out run tests common in many schools. More recently, some coaches and parents have pushed promising young runners to do marathons. Remember, you're just growing up. You've got lots of time to do twenty-six miles when you're older. Try five miles. Maybe six. Then go play soccer. Or even baseball if you don't feel too energetic. Swim. Go fly a kite. It's a nice day.

Eating Right

4

Food. You can't do without it. Mix the right amounts of the right food with the right exercise and you usually come up with a fit person. There's a whole science of what happens to your body after you eat a Big Mac or a raw carrot. It's the science of nutrition. Nutritionists figure out how your body turns food into energy, and which foods do the best job of keeping you healthy.

Here's an example of how knowing something about nutrition can keep you out of trouble when you run. It may be something you've figured out by yourself. But you probably don't know why it's true.

The question: can you gobble down a peanut butter and jelly sandwich and three chocolate chip cookies, chug-a-lug two glasses of milk...and then dash out and run?

The answer: sure, but you won't like it. Food doesn't just drop into your intestines willy nilly. It has to be digested first. After you've eaten, food stays in your stomach anywhere from a half hour to five hours, depending on the food. Fats take the longest.

So if you run right after eating, your body will be fighting one of those little biochemical battles for which it is so famous. The problem is this: your digestive system needs extra blood and oxygen to handle the food. But if you're running, your muscles will be competing for the same blood and oxygen. Neither will work as well as they could if your running and eating had been better timed.

Besides, you could get a cramp in your side, a stitch (see Chapter Five) so it's better to wait two or three hours after eating before running. Many people like to run only when they're hungry—just before breakfast or dinner—when there's absolutely nothing left to digest.

Don't run low on water

For the runner, it's not so bad to be a little hungry. But never be thirsty. When you run, you need water—lots of it. Even if you aren't thirsty before starting to run, have a couple of cups anyway. One doctor suggests this: drink as much as you can. Then force down a little more. You may not need any during a two or three mile run (though it can't hurt, if you see a fountain, to stop and drink) but remember to have a cup when you finish.

The hotter and muggier the weather, the more water you'll need. Drinking water during long races can keep you from getting sick, possibly seriously ill, from heat exhaustion.

Plenty of water may even help your performance. Dr. George Sheehan, the famous physician-marathon runner, says his times are much faster when he stops frequently during a race to drink some water.

You can survive for days without any food; you can drag on for weeks without eating though you'll be in pretty bad shape. But you'll start going downhill quickly if you go even a day without water, and no one can survive without water for more than a few days.

The reason is that more than half of you is water. If you wrung yourself out like a towel, more than half of your

More than half of you is water.

weight would form a puddle on the floor. About 40% is the fluid part of your blood. Some 35% is water inside body cells. And about 25% is water between the cells. Even if you just go to and from home and school, and you don't exercise at all, you replace all of that water every two weeks. If you do exercise, you have to replace that water even faster.

Water has many tasks. For one thing, all the important chemical reactions inside you that make food into energy take place in water. If the body doesn't have enough, everything you do is a little less efficient.

Another of water's key roles is to keep your internal temperature relatively normal (between 98 to 99°F.) no matter how hot or cold it is outside. When you run, your body starts heating up and you begin to sweat. As the sweat evaporates, it cools your body. And that sweat, of course, is water. As long as your body has enough water to keep producing sweat properly, you'll be okay. If your body's dehydrated, there'll be less sweat or none, thus it will be difficult to get your body to regulate its temperature during exercise. If the heat keeps building up, something's got to give. And that will be you.

So, if you're racing or running over ten miles or it's very hot and muggy, make sure you drink before, during and after the run. Stop to drink every two or three miles. Drink more if you stop to do the exercises suggested in Chapter Seven. Drink some then.

One more tip: it's better to drink plain water or fruit juices rather than carbonated soft drinks. The refined sugar in soft drinks actually draws water out of your cells and makes you thirstier.

The other nutrients

By now you know that water is the best thing since running shoes. Luckily—since we have to replace it so often—we also get a lot of water just by eating. Milk and fruit juices are about 90% water; fruits and vegetables about 80%; meats are half water, even bread is about 30%.

Besides, the foods we eat every day are combinations of the other essential nutrients: proteins, carbohydrates, fats, minerals and vitamins. Learn about these nutrients, and you may be able to turn food into the advantage it should be rather than the disadvantage it is for many people.

The idea, once again, is to eat the right amount of the right foods — what's called a balanced diet. This doesn't mean that there is one perfect plan for everyone. It doesn't mean you have to be rigid about what you eat and what you don't. It means that certain classes of food — say fruits or vegetables — are high in some nutrients and low in others.

So, if you want to keep your diet low in protein (12%), relatively low in fats (30%) and relatively high in carbohydrates (58%), which some government scientists suggest, then you'll have to know two things:

1. What *are* carbohydrates, fats and proteins, to say nothing of minerals and vitamins?

2. What foods have how much of what nutrients and how much should you eat?

On page 54, you will find a chart that should answer most

A well-balanced diet combines the essential nutrients: proteins, carbohydrates, fats, minerals and vitamins.

of your questions about the second point. Remember that all this varies depending on your age and how active you are.

Your body's first need is for energy. And food supplies it. A good portion of the fuel you ingest is used for what's called involuntary activities — your heart beat, your digestion and your body's electrical system, to name a few. So you use a lot of energy even if you just lie about in bed all day. All of this involuntary activity is called basal metabolism. In addition to that, you need more fuel when you're active — how much depends on what you're doing. Talking to your sister doesn't take as much energy as running around the block.

Let's look at the main nutrients to see how you get energy.

Carbohydrates: These are our best source of energy, the cheapest and most efficient fuel. One reason is that the body converts them into energy more quickly and easily than fats, the other main source of fuel. You sometimes hear that a candy bar is "quick energy." It can be. But, if it has nuts or chocolate (which are fats), a candy bar can take as long as four hours to digest properly.

It's the sugar in the candy bar that gets into your system fast and gives you energy. Carbohydrates are sugars, which are found in fruits and in regular table sugar, and starches, such as bread, cereal, rice, pasta, potatoes and vegetables. Your body needs these foods constantly to stay alert and for quick reflexes.

If you skip breakfast, it's the lack of carbohydrates that gives you trouble in that last period before lunch. Your brain and nervous system need carbohydrates and going without them for just twelve hours or so starts to cause weakness and dizziness — not to mention hunger.

All carbohydrates are broken down by your liver into a simple sugar called glucose. This is true regardless of whether it is in the form of honey or an apple or spaghetti or broccoli. The glucose — or blood sugar — is taken by the bloodstream to your brain and to your muscles, where it is needed for normal day-to-day activity.

When you have more glucose than you can use right away, a small amount of it is converted to a substance called glycogen, which is first stored in your liver and then in your muscles. It can be used for unusual sustained activity — such as running — or any major exertion lasting more than a few minutes. It's fashionable among marathon runners these days to eat a big spaghetti dinner the night before the race, hoping that their muscles will get an extra shot of glycogen for the long run. This is part of a pre-race eating plan called "carbohydrate loading," and runners claim it helps them push past the well-known twenty-mile barrier ("hitting the wall") of the twenty-six-mile, 385 yard-race.

Some nutritionists, however, say there's no way to store enough glycogen in a runner's muscles from a spaghetti dinner the night before to make such a difference in energy. It's all psychological, they say.

Choosing carbohydrates

Many people try to get most of their carbohydrates from grains, vegetables and fruits. For one thing, the whole grain foods — breads and cereals that have barley, oats or wheat as the base — have a non-digestible substance called fiber. It stimulates your digestive system so that you don't get constipated or have diarrhea. Fiber is also found in fresh fruits and vegetables that haven't been over-cooked.

The refined sugar that's found in baked goods and candy is carbohydrate, too, but it's the kind that catches up to you. What you can handle now may put on weight in a few years. The sugars and starches that your body doesn't use right away and that can't be stored as glyco-gen (because the liver and muscles can handle only a limited amount) turns into adipose tissue, better known as fat. Body fat, that is. Not dietary.

Fats. Dietary fat is your body's second preferred source of energy. But these fats also go a long way in making food taste good. They keep your skin from getting dry and flaky and help your body absorb some important vitamins.

Of course, dietary fat becomes adipose tissue too. Even more fattening than the carbohydrate from a potato or slice of bread is the butter that goes with them. Butter, like most foods made from animal products, has a high fat content. So does whole milk, most cheeses, eggs and beef (see those lines of fat in a steak — the more there are, the tastier the steak).

Fat is, in effect, the body's long-distance energy storer. It's what kept our ancestors alive through long, cold winters with no berries to pick. And if you were locked out of the kitchen for a week, you would soon begin to live off the fat in your adipose tissue. That's why you'd get thinner. Exercise will burn up excess fats too.

Though the body stores energy in fat, it's slow and complicated to use that energy. That's why the body uses carbohydrates first.

The difference in fats

So far, the fat we've mentioned (butter and steak) is solid fat — also known as saturated fat. There's another kind of fat, (invisible to the eye) found in most, but not all, of the same foods — those of animal origin and dairy products. That's called cholesterol and your parents may be trying to reduce the amount of it in their diet. Foods high in cholesterol are milk, meat, cheese and eggs. Most authorities believe both saturated fat and cholesterol are connected to heart disease later in life.

Polyunsaturated fats, which can help reduce cholesterol levels, are found in foods of vegetable origin, like margarine and vegetable oils (corn, safflower). Fish is an exception to the rule since it is of animal origin but has a lot of polyunsaturated fat in it.

Protein. Carbohydrate and fat are preferred sources of energy because protein has to be spared to build and repair tissues. Only when these more efficient sources of energy are used up does protein get into your body's energy game. Actually this can lead to malnutrition. If a starving child in Bangladesh got protein, he'd use it for fuel and still be protein-deficient.

And, contrary to a notion that still prevails some places in this country, a young runner doesn't need a protein booster. Growing young athletes need protein, just as they need other nutrients. You'll get enough of it with a balanced diet. There is no special extra need for protein for strength. It's one of the oldest wrong ideas around — maybe 7,000 years old.

The old Greek coach

It is said to date back to the 5th century, B.C., when Greek wrestlers competed in open-weight class wrestling, much like today's Sumo wrestlers in Japan. Traditionally, Greek wrestlers had been vegetarians. But some sharp coach of the day, realizing that beef would pack on the pounds (because of all that fat), hired a short-order training table chef and two butchers, and the next thing anyone knew there was a run on steak knives at Mount Olympus. But it wasn't for strength. It was for weight — because in open-weight class, a few extra pounds could mean the difference between winning and losing.

Trouble is that people got the wrong idea over the years — that red meat gives athletes special strength. Beef doesn't. What's more, nutritionists now believe Americans eat far too much protein, especially beef with its high fat content. Eggs, chicken, fish, dried beans and even peanut butter are high in protein and better for you than beef — or pork or lamb. Most dairy products are high in protein, too, but those made with skim milk have less fat. Many top runners compete very successfully with only a small amount of meat or cheese in their diets.

Vitamins. These are your body's spark plugs; they are necessary for the reactions that turn food into energy. Although they aren't direct sources of energy, they're activators, there to make a chemical reaction happen.

Vitamin needs are no greater for the kid who spends all

A Well-Balanced Diet

FOOD

Dairy Products
- Milk
- Cheese
- Ice Cream

Meat, Poultry, Fish
or alternatives:
- — Eggs
- — Legumes
- — Peanut Butter

Grains (bread, cereal,
— rice) Potatoes,
Pastas (spaghetti,
noodles, macaroni)

Vegetables
Carrots, Peas, Onions
A: Rhubarb, Pumpkin
Squash, Beets

Asparagus, Broccoli
B. Salad Greens, Spinach,
Tomatoes

Fruits
- — Citrus (orange, grapefruit, tangerine)
- — Apples, Bananas, Strawberries

Fats
- Butter
- Margarine
- Mayonnaise

Sugars
- Sweets
- Desserts

NUTRIENTS	*DAILY REQUIREMENT* *Years 7-10*	*Years 11-14*
High source of protein, calcium, riboflavin (B_2)	2-3 servings	2-3 servings
High source of protein, B vitamins, iron (especially red meats and organ meats.)	3-4 ounces	3-4 ounces
	Alternatives: 2-3 eggs per week or ½ cup dried beans or 2 tablespoons peanut butter is equal to 1 ounce of meat.	
High source of carbohydrate, moderate source of iron and B vitamins. If whole grain, high source of fiber.	4-5 servings	6-7 servings
Moderate source of most vitamins and minerals—yellow vegetables, i.e., carrots, squash, and dark green vegetables, i.e., broccoli, spinach are high in vitamins A and C.	1 serving	1 serving
	2-3 servings	2-3 servings
High carbohydrate high source of vitamins A and C.	1 serving	1 serving
Moderate source of all vitamins and minerals.	1 or more	1 or more
Vegetable fats and oils are a high source of vitamins A, D and K.	Should be regulated and used only to satisfy energy needs.	
	Should be regulated and used only to satisfy energy needs.	

Chart prepared by Angelica Cantlon, M.S.R.D.
Nutrition Consultant, American Health Foundation.

his time reading than for the little dynamo who runs all day long. A well-balanced diet will give you more than enough vitamins of every kind. Also, check the chart on page 54.

Minerals. These aren't direct sources of energy either but there are more than twenty that your body needs. They are chemical regulators. You've heard, for instance, of how the body needs iron to be strong. Well, it's true, particularly for growing people like you. Good sources of iron are liver, leafy vegetables, raisins and dates.

If you're a boy, your body needs about twice as much iron now as it will when you stop growing. When you're older, your body will store iron. But now you're growing very fast. Iron is important in new tissue growth.

The same is true for girls, except that when you start to menstruate you'll need even more iron because of blood loss. And since girls tend to eat less than boys, menstruating girls should try to make sure their diet is relatively high in iron-rich foods.

Most American boys and girls have diets that provide their other daily mineral needs very nicely. Calcium for strong bones, for instance, comes from milk. Sodium and potassium are two minerals that you get a lot of in your diet and most nutritionists think we eat too much sodium in the form of table salt. The habit of salting all our food can lead to high blood pressure—which even children in the U.S. have. High blood pressure leads to heart disease and stroke.

For the runner, sodium and potassium are important. Sodium is the chief mineral lost in sweat (you all know how sweat tastes salty) though it usually isn't a problem except in very hot weather. Potassium plays a major role in the workings of the cells of your muscles, and if you are low on potassium, you may feel weak. Foods that will keep potassium up are potatoes, bananas, apricots and soybeans. One reason that orange juice is good to drink before you run is that it is high in potassium. So is cranberry juice. Or try a blended banana drink.

How much should you eat?

You will have to eat more for your weight than your parents do because a lot of the fuel you take in is used for growth. A calorie is basically a way of measuring the potential energy of food when burned by the body. Vitamins, minerals and water don't have calories because they aren't burned by the body as fuel. You probably won't have to worry about counting calories unless you're overweight.

Running will help if you need to lose a pound or two, but it won't do all the work. You may have to keep your fork and spoon behind your back as well — or eat foods that are less fattening than the ones you crave. But running could be an asset because any exercise — done vigorously and regularly — can decrease your appetite. Not increase it. That's an old wives tale.

How to lose weight*

Running can also help you because it uses up calories. Running a mile, depending on how fast you go, burns up about 100 to 150 calories. If you do a regular two or three miles a day, you'll burn up at least close to 300 calories. However, a pound of body fat equals 3,500 calories. You'll have run three miles a day for almost twelve days to lose that much. This assumes, of course, that you don't add calories by eating more food.

There's some standard advice for people who want to lose weight: exercise more and eat less. That's oversimplified and it's sometimes hard to find the pattern that works for you, but that is the way to shed pounds. Say you chopped off 300 calories a day from your normal intake. It wouldn't take you but six days to lose that pound.

The best way to control your eating is to write down everything you eat for two weeks. Add up the calories. Then find the foods that you can — and will — do without. Remember that the only way to really lose is to do it slowly. Prepare yourself to go without ice cream for a few months. Substitute a low-fat yogurt instead.

*Be sure to see your doctor before beginning a diet.

Find foods that you like and stick with them. Plan ahead. You can bypass that Big Mac, milkshake and french fries if you realize the total caloric content (along with an apple pie dessert) is 1,500 calories. Too much for one meal. Heaven forbid it's a snack.

When should you eat?

You can eat throughout the day if you want to. There's nothing really wrong with snacking. For one thing, children need more food than adults do. But, too often, snacking is an excuse to consume sugar—in the form of cake, candy, or doughnuts—or salt. Potato chips are fried in fat and covered with salt.

Try snacking on fresh fruit or raw vegetables. Peanut butter and bread, cheese and crackers give you protein and carbohydrate. Oatmeal or granola cookies combine dairy products and grain. Save your milk for the afternoon.

A place to start

One way to understand what you are eating is to read package labels. Manufacturers list the ingredients in descending order of quantity. So you can judge what's in a cereal, for instance, even if the label doesn't list the percentage of nutrients and calories.

Most cereals have too much sugar. If it is listed first, second or third, the proportion is too high. Also, try to find a cereal with high fiber content. If you can find one with high fiber and low sugar that tastes good, stick with it.

What are you?

You are what you eat. How many times have you heard that? Within limits, it's true. Food is one of the choices you get to make all your life. What you consume may determine how good you feel, how tired you get and how well you do in school and after school.

Though it seems a little far off now, the food you eat today and the habits you create now may be involved in whether or not you get heart disease or cancer some day. So think a little bit about what you eat.

Calories Used on Various Activities Per Hour

Activity	*cal. per kg. per hr.*
Bicycling (moderate speed)	2.5
Boxing	11.4
Cello playing	1.3
Crocheting	0.4
Dancing	3.8
Dishwashing	1.0
Dressing and undressing	0.7
Eating	0.4
Exercise	
Moderate	3.1
Strenuous	5.4
Horseback riding, trot	4.3
Ironing (5 lb. iron)	1.0
Knitting sweater	0.7
Lying still, awake	0.1
Painting furniture	1.5
Paring potatoes	0.6
Playing ping pong	4.4
Piano playing	1.4
Reading aloud	0.4
Rowing in race	16.0
Running	7.0
Sewing, hand	0.4
Singing in loud voice	0.8
Sitting quietly	0.4
Skating	3.5
Standing	0.5
Sweeping with broom	1.4
Vacuuming	2.7
Swimming (2 mi. per hr.)	7.9
Typewriting rapidly	1.0
Violin playing	0.6
Walking rapidly (4 mi. per hr.)	3.4
Writing	0.4

Aches and Pains

5

Pain hurts and often that's good. Pain is a reliable warning from your body that something's wrong. It may come with a shriek. Or it may be a gentle grumble. But loud or soft, pain gives you a chance to stop whatever you're doing before something worse happens.

If you're a beginning runner, those little aches and pains you feel the morning after a mile or two are messages from your muscles. Your muscles are reporting that they aren't used to being stretched and worked so hard. That's not pain to worry about. That's just a grumble.

When you're first getting your muscles and cardiovascular system in shape, you may have to use all your willpower to force your body to do that extra half mile you set as your goal. That's not the pain we mean. That's just a loud grumble.

But if you've been a runner for a while, and you suddenly feel a sharp pain in the back of your thigh, take it seriously. Pay attention to your body's warning. Slow down. If the pain doesn't go away, stop.

If your knee starts to hurt, listen to your body. Slow down. Or stop.

It's a rare runner who doesn't get blisters now and then. You should know what they mean (possibly your shoes don't fit) and what to do about them.

That musculoskeletal system again

We've already told you that runners worry about bits and pieces of their musculoskeletal system breaking down. Well, it can happen to you, too. Any runner can stress his body too much by overusing it — running too fast, too far or too long. Especially at first. Muscles that are out of shape get tired fast and injure easily. Doing your warm-ups (see Chapter Seven) helps.

Take a look at a picture of muscles and you'll see that they're like heavy rope — the kind you may have climbed in gym class. But your muscles are more versatile than rope. They're elastic. As you call on them for action, they expand and then return to their normal shape.

Your muscles are attached to your bones by tendons. The best known is one named for Achilles, a great warrior in Greek mythology. Achilles, so the legend goes, had but one weakness — his heel. Naturally, his enemies defeated him with an arrow in the heel. And, not surprisingly, the Achilles tendon attaches your big calf muscle to your heel bone.

Unlike muscles, tendons aren't flexible. They don't expand and contract. They are strong connectors. Muscles do the work, not tendons. But your muscles couldn't move your bones if they weren't connected to them. Without your Achilles tendons, your feet would just flop around without any control.

And, without ligaments, so would your knees and ankles. Ligaments are tough bands of fiber that hold your bones together at the joints. They keep your joints held tightly in place, allowing just the motion that nature intended. If you didn't have ligaments you would be able to bend your leg as far forward at the knee as you can flex it backward. Of course, you wouldn't be able to stand up straight, but the things you could do with your leg would be pretty dramatic.

Now we'll tell you what goes wrong most often, how you can recognize what's happening to you, and what you should do if something hurts. You could pull a muscle, strain a ligament, bruise a joint or break a bone. The first two are the most likely.

Muscles: sore, pulled and cramped

It's likely that beginning runners will have sore muscles for awhile because you're calling on the muscle fibers to do a lot more expanding and contracting than they're used to. But they'll adapt and strengthen. Two miles seems an eternity now. Soon it'll be a breeze.

That soreness all over your body is just a gentle grumble of pain. Take a day off, if you want one, but get back out there tomorrow. Every other day is a good way to begin running.

But if you have a muscle pain in a particular part of your leg, it's probably more than just soreness. You may have pulled or strained a muscle.

A pulled muscle means you've torn muscle fibers, often because of poor warm-ups or sudden violent activity that catches a muscle unprepared. It could also be that you are doing too much running—overtraining and abusing your muscles. And some people, because of the way they are built, are just more susceptible to muscle pulls than others.

When you feel a sudden pain in a muscle, slow down or stop running. It won't go away. It will only get worse.

If you pull the muscle in the back of your thigh, you're in a lot of good company. That's the hamstring. It's a frustrating injury because it can take several weeks to heal properly. You can walk okay and sometimes jog easily with a pulled hamstring, but it hurts to run. And if you reinjure it, it just takes longer to heal.

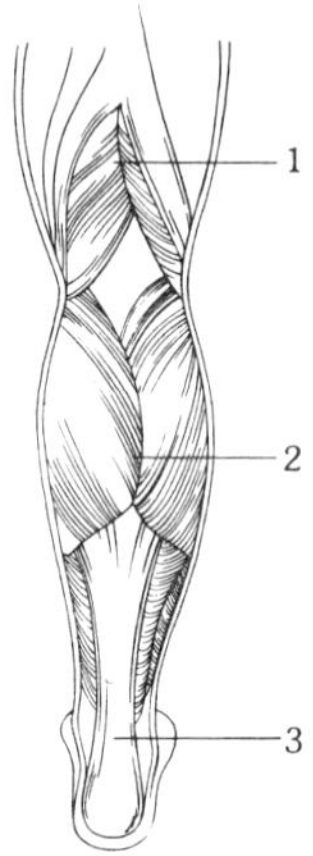

1. Hamstrings
2. Calf muscles
3. Achilles tendon

What to do

- You can help it by putting ice on and off for the first twenty-four hours.
- Wrap an elastic bandage around the pulled muscle.
- If there's swelling, elevate your leg.
- Then, starting about forty-eight hours after the injury, put a heating pad over the spot where it hurts. Heat improves circulation to the injured muscle, which most

doctors think helps it heal faster.

Cramps

You can also get muscle cramps (often called a Charlie horse). Some people seem to get them all the time, more than others do, but if you get them, you'll know it. They are sudden, painful contractions of a muscle. Sometimes they last for just a second or two. Sometimes, you're not so lucky.

Cramps have several causes, among them (and especially for beginning runners) plain, old fatigue. If you continue to get too tired from running, cut back. You're probably trying to do too much. If extreme fatigue persists, see your doctor.

Another common cause of cramps is not enough minerals (salt, potassium and magnesium) in your system. That's why some people get them on hot days when they're sweating a lot, losing the minerals along with the sweat. If you get cramps, some doctors recommend that you eat more fruit and vegetables to get extra potassium into your system (see Chapter Four).

One way to get rid of cramps in the calf of your leg, which is a common place for runners to get them, is to just reach down and squeeze your leg where it hurts. It usually does the trick in a minute or so. Another way is to slowly stretch the calf muscles (see Chapter Seven).

Broken bones and chuckholes

If you do your warm-up exercises properly, and don't outrun your body's limits, you might never have a serious injury. But you never know when you'll step into a chuckhole. It can happen to anybody. You could even fracture an ankle, though runners are rarely victims of broken bones.

Bones have the flexibility of wood and the strength of cast iron. But even a bone can be bent too much. That step into a chuckhole can twist your foot and ankle suddenly and with great force. And your ankle may break. Actually, what breaks is the bottom end of either of the two long bones in your lower leg, the fibula or tibia.

It's more likely, though, that you will sprain your ankle. And a bad sprain can cause you nearly as much trouble as a fracture. (A *sprain* is an injury to a ligament and a *strain* is an injury to a muscle.) The more experienced a runner you are, the less likely that it will be a bad sprain. Running—particularly uphill—toughens your ligaments.

As you run, ligaments keep your bones from flying apart. When you step in a chuckhole, the ligament in your ankle tries to keep the joint together. But the force of your ankle twisting at a crazy angle may be too much even for the tough ligament. Some of its fibers tear or overstretch, and that's a sprain.

Sprains

If you do sprain your ankle, you'll know it. It will hurt a lot and there will be swelling. And, almost certainly, it will not happen unless your leg is twisted somehow in a fall or a trip. And, don't forget, if you fall down, you can sprain your wrist or fingers, bruise your elbow or injure your shoulder. It's possible to do so, but runners hardly ever sprain their knees or hips.

Take sprains very seriously. Ignore them and you may have trouble with your ankle, or whatever you sprain, for the rest of your life. Limp home. Tell your parents. Don't walk on it if you can avoid it. Ask people to bring things to you. Ice cream won't hurt. It won't help, but it won't hurt.

What to do

- It may not be a sprain, but don't take any chances.
- Put ice on the spot where it hurts.
- Rest your leg on a chair or sofa—elevate it.
- Put an elastic bandage on it, but not too tight.
- If the pain doesn't go away in twenty-four hours, it's a good idea to see a doctor.

Just like a broken bone, a bad sprain may require a cast for several weeks. Many doctors, however, just tape the ankle and make the runner as comfortable as possible.

After a cast, it takes weeks before a leg is in shape to run. With a taped ankle, the runner can keep his heart in condition by walking, climbing stairs or bicycling.

You may have just strained muscles in the area of the joint, or bruised it, but any injury to a joint can cause problems. If you have any persistent pain — even if it isn't much — see a doctor.

Remember, pain is telling you something. It's giving you a message that something is wrong. It's rare but you might be short of breath a lot and have pains in your chest. Let the doctor figure out what's causing it. Moderate running shouldn't hurt.

Runner's knee

Runner's knee simply means pain surrounding the kneecap. More than half the time, it results from doing too much, pushing too hard — overuse again. Another related cause is muscle imbalance (see Chapter Seven). If, for instance, your hamstring muscles are tight and you take long strides, your knees will bend more, stressing the muscles, bones and soft tissue in the front of the knees.

Structural malformations in your leg can also cause runner's knee. A bow-legged runner who tries to run straight has to turn his feet inward. This flattens the foot and causes the tibia bone to rotate, which stresses the knee. More pain.

What to do

- If you're bow-legged, find a good coach. He can help correct your running form and improve your training methods to get rid of the pain.
- Be sure that you're doing exercises to strengthen muscles in the front of your legs and stretch those in back.
- To reduce the pain, put ice bags on your knee and use an elastic bandage to keep the kneecap and soft tissue from vibrating back and forth.

Remember the preventive measures: good shoes, soft surfaces, run slowly and easily, do your warm-ups and vary your running route. If it's a structural problem, what most doctors recommend are special shoe inserts, called orthotics, that keep your foot from turning inward too much. They're neat, simple and effective.

Another cause is an abnormal fold in the kneecap, which only a doctor can diagnose.

Watch those tendons

The first thing to remember about tendons is that you are much less likely to injure them if you do the right warm-ups before running. They are usually injured when you sprain an ankle.

The second thing to remember about tendons is that it's easier to hurt them than muscles because they are smaller and less protected.

And the third thing to remember is that if you injure a tendon, you probably won't feel like running for awhile. Still, unless you really injure a tendon about as bad as a tendon can be hurt, it's not as dramatic as a ligament injury. You won't get ice cream just for the asking!

THE ACHILLES TENDON

The Achilles tendon connects the two major muscles in your lower leg to your heel. And because the Achilles tendon is so important to running, it is, naturally, the one you're most likely to injure.

If you suffer a small tear in your Achilles tendon, you'll feel pain in the back of your heel and a little bit above it. And you shouldn't run until the tendon heals. You'll know it has healed if you try running and it doesn't hurt. Some take a long time, as much as several weeks. Let the doctor decide when you should begin running again.

What to do

- Improving your flexibility with gentle stretching of the tendon is the best therapy.
- An ice bag will help.
- Another good remedy is to wear a lift in your running shoes (about a half to three-quarters inch) until you

feel better. In effect, this rests your heel when you run.

A complete tear of the Achilles tendon is much more serious and, fortunately, not too common. Known as a rupture, it occurs when the tendon tears completely away from the bone or from the muscle. If you get a tendon rupture, you're likely to hear a loud "pop" and you'll be in a lot of pain. You won't be able to walk. Get somebody to call a doctor, and get somebody else to find some ice to put on the spot where it hurts.

If left alone, the Achilles tendon would heal by itself but it might be too long and thus, weakened. One treatment is to put it in a cast. But you might be better off to have a complete rupture repaired surgically. It will make your leg better quicker because the surgeon can make sure the tendon is not too long.

TENDINITIS

There's one other tendon problem that can occur and that's tendinitis — an inflammation of the tendon ('itis' is what doctors add on to a word to mean inflamed). In some people their leg muscles get so tight from running that the muscles pull at their tendons. This causes the tendon to get inflamed.

It's very painful if you try to run hard with tendinitis.

What to do

- Rest is the best remedy, allowing the muscles to relax a little.
- Then begin to slowly stretch the tendon.
- Some doctors say you can keep running with tendinitis, but at a very slow jog – as long as it doesn't hurt.
- You may need a compression pad around the place where it hurts you.

SPECIAL DISEASES

Some youngsters can be susceptible to disease where the tendons attach to bones at the heel and knees. These places, called apophyses, are involved with growing and thus are similar to the growth plates we talked about in

Chapter Three.

It isn't that running causes the swelling and sensitivity at the apophyses. But if you feel a dull pain, especially around the knee or the heel, while running, it might be a result of diseases that have nothing to do with exercise. Girls between eleven and fourteen and slightly older boys are prone to Osgood-Schlatter's disease, which is an irritation of the tendon at the tibia, just below the kneecap. The apophysis of the heelbone also can be affected. See your doctor. He can tell by x-ray whether it's a disease that's causing the pain.

If these diseases do occur, it's probably a good idea to curtail your running until you're more comfortable.

Mysterious side stitch

Just about everyone has gotten a cramp in the side while running. Doctors have never known what causes these mysterious side stitches, though rare is the doctor who won't guess. What doctors do know is that they aren't dangerous.

What to do

- If you get one, the first thing to try is to change speed.
- Try slowing down first.
- Dr. Gabe Mirkin, a marathoner and sports medicine specialist, says you should push your fingers into your side where it hurts, lean forward as you run, and breathe out with your lips pursed as if you were whistling.

He believes that side stitches are mostly caused by a cramp of the diaphragm,

Mysterious side stitch.

which is the large, flat muscle that helps you breathe, or the intercoastal muscles, which help elevate the ribs when you're breathing hard.

As we've said, eating before you run causes a conflict between your digestive tract and your muscles. If you eat just before your run, both require large amounts of blood, and neither do the best job of which they are capable.

The side stitches may be a result of that biochemical spat between your digestion and your muscles. The diaphragm isn't getting enough blood as you breathe harder with all the exercise, and it complains via a stitch in your side. Remember, listen to your body. It's telling you things. All you have to do is figure out what it's saying.

What to do

- But you can minimize the pain by cutting down on your running for awhile.
- Go slower. Do fewer miles.
- Avoid running downhill and sharp turns.
- Don't take long strides.
- Try wearing elastic stockings on your legs when you run. Some doctors say they give you just enough compression for the bones and muscles to relax.
- Use ice packs in-between runs.
- Make sure your shoes give you proper cushioning and support.

Shin splints

Naturally, the worst thing you can do to one of your bones is to break it. But you runners can have some other problems with your legs and feet as well. After all, you take thousands of steps when you run five miles. That's a lot of pounding on two feet.

Shin splints are another of those conditions that doctors argue about all the time. Nobody really knows why some people, some of the time, have pain in the front of their legs—from knee to ankle—when they run. Some runners say they only get shin splints when they run on pavement. But other runners never run on pavement, and they still get shin splints now and then. Some people run on pavement all the time, and they never get shin splints.

First, don't worry about shin splints. You can keep running as long as the pain isn't bad. The most common cause is all that pounding. It's too much in too short a time, and your bones and muscles can't tolerate it. Another possible cause is muscle imbalance. Other doctors think it's from a tight Achilles tendon or weak ankles and feet. In such instances, orthotics might help.

If the pain continues when you run, stop. Shin splints generally get better with rest. In the meantime, keep yourself in condition by swimming, bicycling or skipping rope.

Once the shin splints are gone, doctors recommend exercises to strengthen the muscles in the front of your leg. Another suggestion is to walk on your heels for awhile. This stretches the muscles around your shin and also the Achilles tendon.

Stress fractures

If your shin splints don't get better in a couple of weeks, they may not be shin splints. The pain you are having could be a stress fracture. You need to have an x-ray to know for sure.

Stress fractures are tiny cracks in the surface of bones, sometimes in the front of the tibia bone and often in the small bones of your feet.

Like shin splints, they usually don't hurt when you're walking, but they do when you run. And, like shin splints, they heal with rest—no casts are needed.

What to do

- First, minimize the pain by easing up on your running.
- Don't run on hard surfaces.
- If it doesn't disappear, stop for awhile but do exercises that won't irritate the injury. Some doctors recommend walking uphill for awhile, instead of running.

- Runners also get stress fractures in the feet. Taping the foot or special thick-soled running shoes with an arch support can help stop the pain.

Plantar fascia

Runner's feet take a terrible pounding. They wouldn't hold out at all if it weren't for an amazing sheet of fibrous tissue on the soles of your feet that cushions the muscles and bones of your feet from the shock of thousands of running steps. It's called the plantar fascia.

Trouble is, runners can get a painful condition called plantar fascitis (inflammation of the fascia) that will stop you right in your tracks.

It starts with a small tear in the fascia. At first, you probably won't even notice the problem. But within a few days, it develops gradually into a more serious tear, and *then* you notice it. The pain is usually in the heel, but it can be anywhere on the sole of your feet.

What to do

- The treatment is rest.
- But you can prevent it in the first place by starting to run slowly and gradually add more time and miles. Avoid intense training.
- Don't turn sharply when running.
- Invest in good shoes that give proper support and have soles that aren't too stiff.
- Run on soft surfaces rather than hard.

Got a blister?

Don't be surprised if you get blisters on your feet, no matter how long you've been running. A new pair of shoes, different socks, almost anything can, at one time or another, lead to a blister.

Blisters are simply fluid that has collected in the outer part of the skin, usually the result of persistent and repeated rubbing by shoe or sock. Make sure your sock doesn't bunch up. Good-fitting shoes are your best protection. If your shoes are new, and they haven't been broken in just right yet, rub some Vaseline on the shoe where it's been chafing your foot.

If you want to drain the blister by puncturing it with a needle, sterilize the needle over a flame first (don't burn your finger holding the needle). Then, after the needle has cooled, puncture the blister at the edge, and drain the fluid by pressing the top of the blister. But don't remove the skin. Use an antiseptic, and cover it with a bandage. Blisters can get infected.

Keeping your feet clean and dry helps prevent infection. It also helps prevent athlete's foot, which can afflict anyone, athlete or not. It's called athlete's foot because the fungus that causes scaliness and cracks between the toes thrives on just those dark, wet places. And athletes often have sweaty feet.

There are some remedies at the drug store, but the best advice is to keep your feet dry when you're not running and your socks clean.

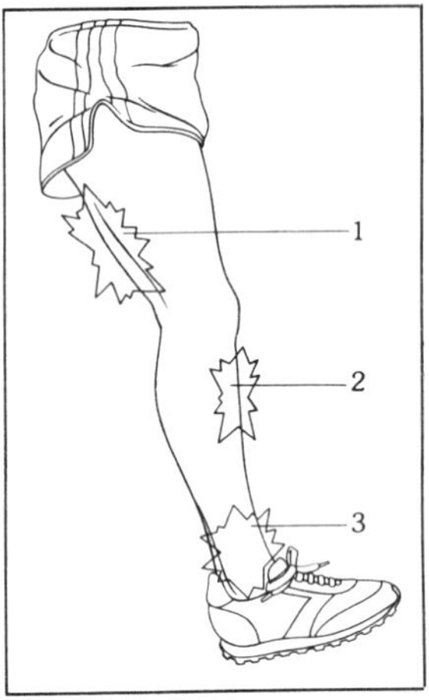

1. Pulled hamstring
2. Shin splints
3. Sprain

Heat Problems

Aside from those chuckholes, your worst enemy when running is the sun. The heat and the humidity, actually. You can run into heat problems when the temperature's only 70° but the humidity is 95%. The wind plays a role, too. It's easier to keep cool if there's a breeze.

HEAT CRAMP

If it's been hot for several days, and you've been running, a heat cramp is not unheard of. They're just like ordinary cramps and you can get one anywhere in your body. Sit down in the shade for awhile. Massage the cramp. Then

go home, make some lemonade and sit under a big tree — if one's handy — for the rest of the afternoon. You're probably dehydrated and need fluid and, perhaps, salt. Salting your food at dinner will most often take care of replacing what you lost. If cramps persist, see a doctor.

Sit down, and massage the cramp in your calf.

HEAT EXHAUSTION

Heat exhaustion is more common. The runner can get confused and feel fuzzy. His skin may be wet and clammy, his face pale. Some runners have even passed out from heat exhaustion. Get into the shade or a cool area. Drink water or some other cool liquid. Tell your doctor what happened.

The best way to avoid heat exhaustion is to be sure your body is used to the hot weather. During the first few days of a heat wave, run less and slower. Run in the shade. Run in the cool part of the day — early morning or early evening.

HEAT STROKE

Heat stroke is relatively rare. But dangerous. The runner may vomit or not be able to talk clearly. He may be flushed, with dry skin. His temperature may be elevated. He may be dizzy. If this happens, get him to a shady area, rub water or ice on him if possible. Most important, call an ambulance. Right away. Get him to a hospital as soon as you can.

SCARED YOU OFF?

Now that you know the dread things that can happen to a runner, have we scared you off? We doubt it. Actually, running is one of the safest sports around, but it never hurts in life to know the pitfalls.

Shoes, Suits and Sites

6

Shoes. Do running shoes really matter? Wouldn't it be okay to run in sneakers? Well, the answers are first, yes. And, then, no.

Our primitive ancestors ran around in bare feet, but they were running on soft earth and grass. And their feet were tough from a lifetime of walking and running barefoot. For most of us, running shoes are necessary.

When you run, your foot strikes the ground with about three times the force you put there when you're walking. And chances are, the ground you're striking is hard. Without adequate cushioning you may injure your foot and calf muscles. The trouble is that tennis shoes, sneakers or basketball shoes just don't give you enough cushioning to prevent problems in the long run. They might do when you start running. But if you stick with it, you'll soon want regular running shoes.

So, okay, how do you choose the *right* running shoes for you? If you've ever been in a sports store, you know there are now hundreds of different running shoes. Blunt, narrow, wide, with winged heels, without winged heels, red, purple, canvas, nylon, yellow, pink.

What to do

Well, you can choose the color to match your baby blue eyes if you want, and you can go with whatever fabric feels and looks good to you. You might read the annual shoes issue of running magazines for help. But better still:

- Try on running shoes toward the end of the day when your feet are a little swollen, the way they'll be when you've run half a mile. And wear your running socks.

- Walk around in the shoes—bounce a little, see how they feel. They should feel snug, not tight. Be sure you have enough room for your toes—about three-quarters of an inch from the end of your toes to the tip of the shoe.

- The sole should be thick enough to cushion your running, but not so thick that it strains your muscle as you bend your toes. Test this by bending the toe of the shoe backward when it's off your foot. If you can't bend it back easily, try another brand.

• The heel — which is where your foot lands when you're running — needs to be very resilient to absorb the shock. Test it with your hand. Also, the heel should be about three inches wide for extra stability.

Take your time to see how both shoes feel. Think. Don't let the salesperson push you. Running shoes are expensive, but they're your only piece of equipment. Good, comfortable running shoes will do more than anything else to make running a real pleasure. Find the shoes that suit *you*. Feet are quite different and no one running shoe is best for all feet.

A good running shoe must have a thick sole to cushion your running and a resilient heel to absorb shock.

Suiting up for the weather

The rest of your gear is easier to put together. In fact, you may not have to buy anything to assemble two outfits — one for warm and one for cold weather running. You just have to follow a few common-sense rules.

If you understand how your body heats itself up and cools itself down, then the rules we're talking about really will seem like — well — common sense.

Your body is a self-regulating furnace keeping its temperature at about 98.6°F., whatever you're doing and whatever temperature it is outside. When you run — whatever the weather — your body produces a lot of extra heat. Your circulation system brings that heat to the surface of the skin. In the summer, you want to get rid of the extra heat. In the winter, you want to retain it.

When the outside temperature is high, or the humidity is, your body picks up heat from the environment. So, when you run in hot and muggy weather, it's more difficult for your body to maintain its equilibrium. And, at least one doctor thinks that children are more susceptible to heat and humidity because most are smaller than adults. Children have more skin compared to their body than grown-ups do and thus, take in more heat from the environment.

As we told you in Chapter Four, evaporation of sweat is the way your body cools itself. Water is sent to the surface of the skin and the outside temperature evaporates it, causing you to feel — and be — cooler. A good wind helps, as does the breeze you create by running. Low humidity also helps the evaporation of sweat. (Try wetting your hand, then blowing on it to understand the effect.) What you need to do — the basis of the common-sense rules — is to make the sweating mechanism as efficient as possible. You can do that by:

- Making sure you drink plenty of liquids — water and fruit juices are good — before you begin your run. And drink some more during your run if you feel thirsty or tired.

- Running in the morning or evening when it's cooler and in the shade if you can. Like the song says, "only mad dogs and Englishmen go out in the midday sun." Ease up during the first of a heat wave so that your body gets used to the weather. Run slower and shorter distances for the first few days. You should be able to resume your regular schedule by the third or fourth day. And, in any hot weather, drink lots of fluid, more than you want or think you need. Lemonade is very good. So is just plain water.

- Wearing a light colored hat, not too tight, with a wide brim or a visor, maybe your baseball cap, to keep the sun off your head and face.

Protect yourself from the sun by wearing a hat.

- Wearing a white or pale colored, cotton T-shirt that fits well. White to reflect heat. Cotton because it's light and absorbs sweat—unlike dacron, nylon, acrylic and other artificial fibers, which don't. They make you hotter. The close fit (not *tight*) lets your sweat be immediately absorbed by the shirt and then dried by the heat and the breeze. If the shirt is loose, the cooling takes place a few inches from the skin.

The kind of shorts you wear really aren't important, but you'll be most comfortable if they're light-colored, cotton and don't chafe. If they chafe, try a different kind, or a different size. If you have big thighs, give them room.

Dressing for the cold

In cold weather, as we said, you want to retain that extra

heat you generate by running. The simple way to do that is by:

- Wearing wool and cotton clothes—including wool socks—because these fabrics are warmer, even when wet, than man-made materials.

- Dressing in layers so that air gets trapped between the layers and can act as insulation against the cold. First a cotton undershirt and long johns, then a light wool sweater and shorts and, if it's very cold, a heavier sweater or windbreaker and sweatpants as a final layer. Wear whatever feels good.

- Wearing a kerchief around your neck to keep out cold breezes and wearing a hat to keep in the 70% of body heat that experts say escapes via your head—when you *don't* wear a hat.

Layering is the best way to dress in cold weather because as you run and warm up, you can take off the kerchief and open your windbreaker or take off a sweater. Then when the sun goes in, you can zipper back up.

Another thing to remember in cold weather: the wind chill factor is important. Start your run *into* the wind because it's colder and you'll warm up through running. On your return, you'll have the wind behind you (to push you). If it's *really* cold, test yourself out with a short run before you commit yourself to your goal of two or three miles or whatever.

One extra point for older girls: some sports medicine experts recommend that you wear a bra for running, even if you don't everyday, to help prevent breast tissue breakdown. If you feel your breasts are bouncing around too much, then wear one. It's really up to you.

Where to run

Tarton—what tracks are made of—is the best surface to run on, dry grass is next best, then earth. They cushion your footfall, but they're not so soft that they absorb the energy your legs are generating to push you forward.

Concrete and pavement are hard but your running is more efficient on them. Choose pavement over concrete if you have to make the choice.

Though your school running track may be an ideal surface, it's often boring running round and round in a circle.

Avoid running along roads that carry heavy traffic. Unless there's a stiff breeze the air is likely to be so polluted that it's a real hazard to your health. Much depends on how the breeze is blowing—which direction—but try to stay at least sixty feet from highways. If you must run on roadways, run facing the oncoming traffic.

Frankly, we recommend not running at night. It's just plain dangerous. But if you ever have to, wear light-colored clothes, or, better yet, a reflective pullover (like bicyclers wear) that will reflect car headlights.

If you can run where there are trees, fresh air, some birds and flowers, then that's the place to experience the true pleasure of running.

Dry grass is best. Concrete and pavement can be hard on your legs and feet.

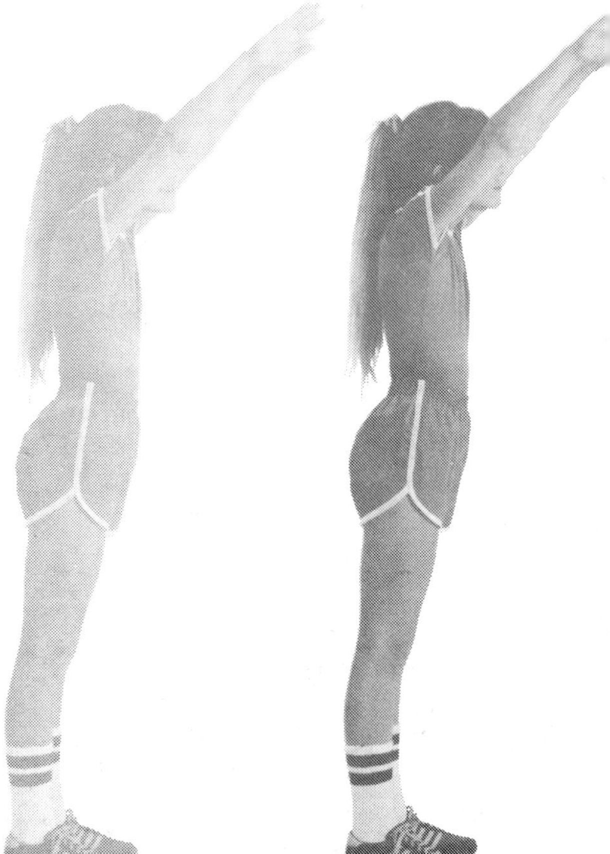

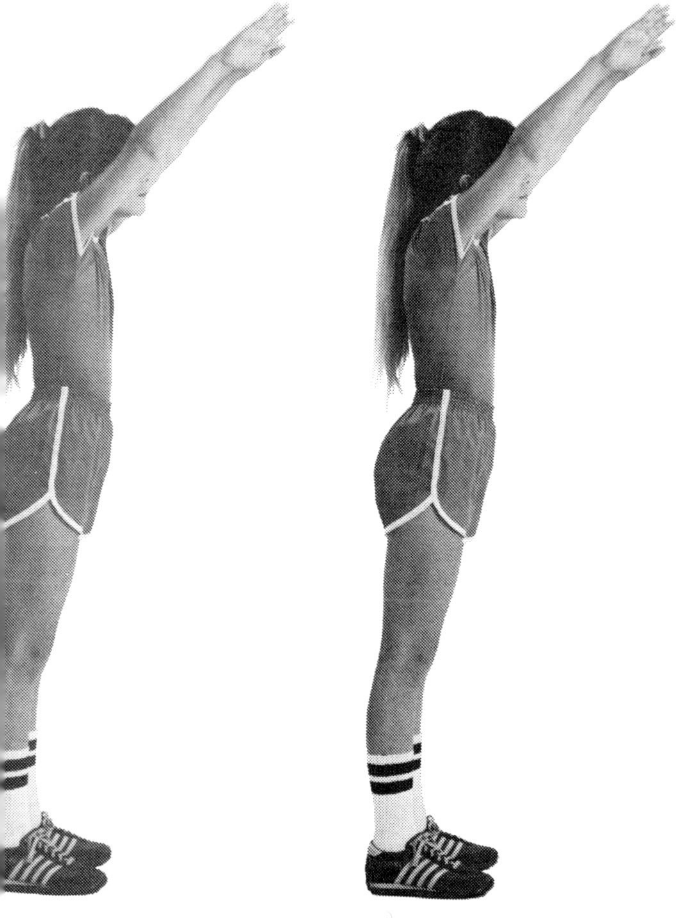

When a pitcher allows two doubles, a triple, a home run, and a walk and there are still no outs, no doubt something's going on in the bullpen. The coach orders another pitcher to warm up.

From Little League to the majors, pitchers have to warm up before taking the mound. If they don't, they can hurt their arms.

Well, it's the same for runners. You have to warm up before taking to the track or to the countryside. If you don't, you can hurt your legs. Remember the chapter on how bits and pieces of your musculoskeletal system can get overused? Stretching exercises keep your muscles from losing their flexibility and help prevent muscle tears.

Calling extra blood

When we say warm up, we mean it. Warm-ups get extra blood flowing to muscles you plan to use the most, and that gets them warmer. When they're warmer, they work more efficiently and are less susceptible to injury.

When muscles are flexible, they're much less likely to get hurt. Stick a leather shoe in the freezer, and a couple of hours later it's frozen stiff. But if you warm it with your hands for a while, it gets nice and soft again. Bend the toes back and forth—that's like a warm-up exercise. But only for shoes. Not you.

Different exercises stretch different muscles. So you can't just touch your toes ten times and consider yourself warmed up.

The muscles that get the tightest in runners are, naturally, the ones that do the hardest work; the hamstrings in the back of the thighs and the calf muscles in the lower leg. What running warm-ups do is stretch these tight muscles and prepare the joints for action.

Warm-ups have to be done gradually at first. You have to give your body time to adjust to a heavier workload.

Running isn't everything

By now, you may have gotten the idea that running is all you need to get fit and stay fit. Sorry. There's more — not too much more, but more. Running doesn't do much for your upper-body strength. You will need to do other exercises to build up strong arms and shoulders.

So, if you want to be fit from head to toe, it is necessary to do some strengthening exercises after the warm-ups or even at some other time. Some people like to stop midway in a run to do them. So, we'll describe some strengthening exercises that'll help you, say, climb a rope — if you ever need to in an emergency. Who knows when you'll be trapped half way up a mountain?

And... there's one thing more. No matter how faithful you are with your warm-ups, you will have to add some strength-building exercises to balance the development of calf muscles and hamstring muscles. If not, the weak muscles in front can be overpowered — it's called imbalance — and possibly injured because there's a delicate balance in your leg when you move. Whenever a muscle moves in one direction, another has to move in the opposite direction. That one should be equally strong. We'll give you a few exercises to help strengthen these potentially weak muscles.

Do it yourself

There's no magic to the warm-ups in the next few pages. You may know of some other good ones, too. But the ones we're going to give you are a bare minimum for most of you. You can move the order around.

But keep in mind that you've got to stretch the muscles that running strengthens (primarily the calf, hamstrings and back muscles) and strengthen weak muscles (those around the shin, thigh and stomach in particular), and also your arms and shoulders.

Stretching exercises are usually done as warm-ups preparatory to running and later during a cool-down period. But there's one thing more. Once you've done the warm-up exercises, don't just head out at a full gallop. Walk slowly, then briskly for a few minutes and move gradually into jogging, increasing your speed easily to a comfortable pace. This helps to prepare your heart and circulatory system for a heavier workload.

When you have completed a run, you should do the same routine but in reverse order. Don't just flop on the ground. Walk for several minutes to cool down and select some of your favorite stretching exercises to complete the workout.

Okay? Ready to go?

Stretching exercises

BUTTERFLY STROKE — This exercise loosens shoulder joints and surrounding muscles. Stand with your feet a few inches apart, bend forward slightly, stretch out both arms to your sides, and rotate your arms in large circles at the same time, much like the butterfly stroke in swimming. Beginners should do this exercise about ten times, gradually increasing the number to twenty as the days go on.

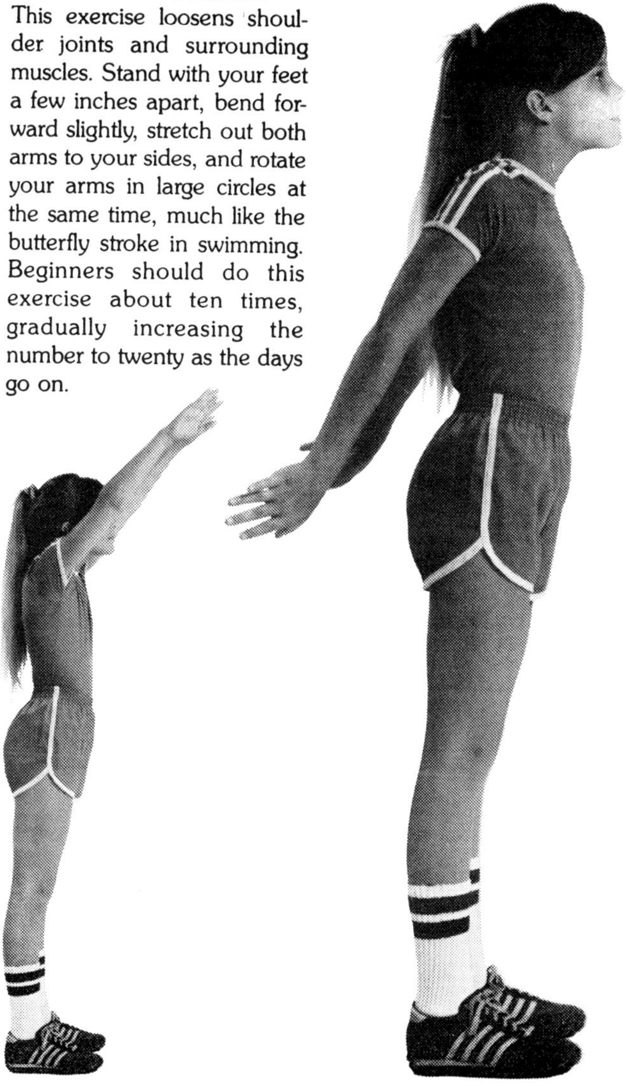

NECK ROTATION—This is good for your upper body and helps to relax the muscles in your neck. Rotate your head slowly to the right and then to the left and repeat. Nod your head forward and back. And slowly swing your head in a full circle, first one way then the other. Beginners might do this exercise about five times each way.

PUSH AWAY—Face a tree or a wall and reach out to place your hands flat against the tree (wall). Keep your heels on the ground and your toes pointed straight ahead and slowly bending your elbows, move closer to the tree. Keeping your legs straight stretches the calf muscles and the Achilles tendons. You should feel a little pressure in these areas. If you don't feel it, you're probably too close to the tree (wall) and need to move your feet back. When you feel the pressure, hold the stretch for five seconds. Count 1,000 and one, 1,000 and two...then relax. Repeat three times.

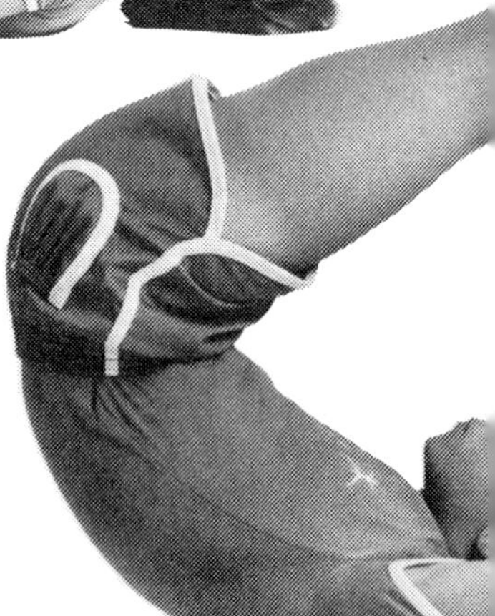

BACKOVER — This is a good stretching exercise for your lower back. Lie on your back, and lift your legs up over your head with your knees straight. Try to touch the ground behind you with your toes. Hold for fifteen seconds. Bend your knees, relax, return to starting position and repeat several times.

STANDING LEG STRETCH—This one is good for stretching the hamstrings and back muscles. Find a park bench (or, if you're home, a table will do) and raise one leg high to the back of the bench. Keep the other foot on the ground pointed straight ahead. Slowly extend your fingertips toward the outstretched leg on the table. With time you may be able to touch your forehead to your knee. Do each leg twice, holding for fifteen seconds each time.

HAMSTRING STRETCHER — Still another exercise for stretching the hamstring muscles. Stand up. Cross one leg in front of the other. Slowly bend forward from the waist and hips to touch the toes, keeping your rear leg straight and holding the heel to the ground. Relax and bend forward easily. Hold for fifteen seconds. Change forward leg. Repeat several times.

HURDLER'S STRETCH — This is an alternative exercise for stretching the hamstring muscles. Sit on the floor or the ground. Extend the right leg forward and fold the left leg under your buttocks. Reach forward and touch the right foot with the left hand. Repeat about ten times. Change legs and repeat.

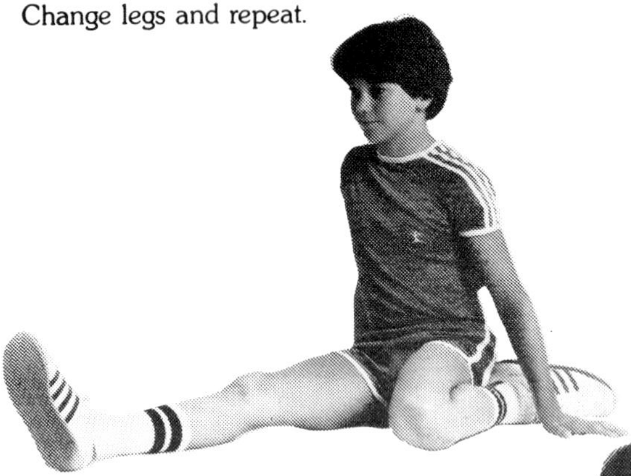

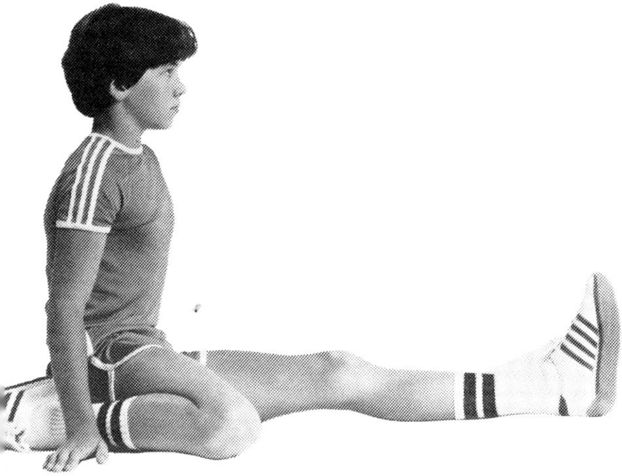

HIP FLEXOR—This is a good exercise for stretching the muscles that flex your hip. Lie on your stomach (you can do this one before you go to sleep or after you wake up if you want). Lift one foot and reach behind you to grab it on the ankle. One at a time. Bend your knee and carefully pull your leg in and hold for five seconds. Don't rotate your knee to the side. Do each leg twice.

LOW BACK STRETCH—This exercise stretches the muscles in your lower back and buttocks. You can also do this one in bed. Lie down on your back. Pull your knees to your chest. You can do one leg at a time or both together. If you leave one leg lying flat, the muscles that flex the hip are stretched too. Hold for five seconds. Release your knees and relax. Then do four times.

Strengthening exercises

FLUTTER KICKS—This strengthens the muscles in your lower back and buttocks. Lie flat on your stomach. (You might do this one in bed, also.) Put your arms under your thighs. Tense the muscles in your buttocks. Then raise your legs and do some flutter kicks. (No bending the knees.) Do ten to twenty, if you can. But don't strain.

PUSH-UPS — This exercise strengthens your arms, shoulders and lower back. You may not be able to do many regular push-ups at first. If not, start with a modified version — with your knees touching the ground. That way, you're only pushing up part of your body weight. If you work out regularly, you'll soon be doing them with your arms and shoulders supporting all your weight, with only toes and hands touching the ground. This position has your toes curled under and your hands placed at shoulder width. Then you push up until your arms are fully extended, keeping your body straight from head to toe. No lifting your rear end above the rest of your body. Try ten. Some people can do dozens.

SIT-UPS — This exercise can build strong stomach muscles. Lie on your back, hands clasped behind head or arms extended overhead, knees bent and feet or heels flat on ground, close to your buttocks, then curl up into a sitting position. If necessary, your feet can be held by a friend or hooked under a stationary object. Up down, up down — maybe twenty times. If these are too tough, grab your thighs as you curl up. Eventually, you'll be able to do sit-ups without such help. You can get a heavier workout by clasping your hands behind your neck. A popular variation is to twist your trunk touching elbows to opposite knees.

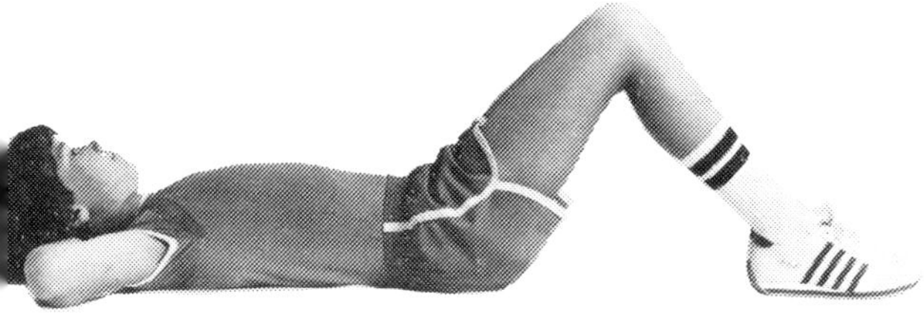

HANG-UPS AND CHIN-UPS — These are good for your arms and shoulders. Hang by your hands from something you are sure won't break. Be careful of tree limbs. It's easier if you grasp the tree or bar with your palms toward you. Slowly rotate your body in both directions. Don't strain. Then, if your arms and shoulders are strong enough, pull your body by your hands until your chin is at the level of your hands. Do as many as possible without straining.

SITTING TUCKS — This is good for strengthening your stomach muscles. Sit down. Put your hands flat on the ground by your buttocks or hips. Lift your legs up and bend your knees. Wrap your arms around them. Then extend your legs out in front of you and arms overhead. Repeat four or five times. It may be hard to maintain your balance at first. Practice makes perfect.

HALF-SQUAT — This is good for strengthening your quadriceps and buttocks muscles. Place your hands on your hips. Extend arms forward and bend your knees to a half-squat position (thighs parallel to the ground). Hold momentarily, then rise slowly to an upright position. Repeat eight to ten times.

Gait

8

Most of you have run round the block at one time or another in your lives. Running is no stranger. Everybody knows how to do it. But the type of running we're talking about is a little different. It's distance running—three, four, or five miles, maybe even more.

When you're running for a first down playing football, it's just ten or fifteen yards. Even if you hit a homer, it's just 120 yards. When you chase a Frisbee, it's just a few steps.

But when you run a couple of miles, it's thousands of steps. And if you're doing some little thing wrong, it can add up. You won't have a problem at twenty yards if you lean too far forward. But two miles is 3,520 yards. You might scrape your nose. Running with good form will make you a happier runner.

It may be hard to believe, but a lot of people don't know how to run properly. The position of their arms and feet or the way they bend forward as they run may be wasting energy. Running wrong may cause blisters or even aches and pains (see Chapter Five). Good form will make sure you go farther and faster with the same amount of energy.

The right gait

Now that we've gotten that across, here's something that will make you wonder why you read the page at all. There's no running form that's good for everyone. Some people lope gracefully. Others plod along like a tank. If you're short and stocky, don't try to imitate your tall, lanky friend. It won't work.

But some general guidelines about running may keep you on the right path.

- Your toes should land in the direction you are heading, not angled off to the right or left. That's easiest on your feet and ankles—and it saves you distance.

- Don't land on the balls of your feet as if you were dashing down the street after your brother. Land closer to flat footed, rolling forward, and pushing off with your toes.

• Run tall. Think of your weight over your feet. Imagine a straight line that goes from the top of your head to your feet. Keep your back straight, your head up. By this, we don't mean that you should be rigid as you run. Watch distance runners like Bill Rodgers or Frank Shorter on TV sports shows. You'll see what we mean. In fact, you'll probably work out a comfortable gait on your own without our help.

• Keep your knees slightly bent as you run. Don't overstride.

• Don't let your arms flop out to your side when you run—the so-called "running-like-a-girl" posture. Your arms should pump easily and close to your body, elbows bent and relaxed.

• Try to keep your shoulders level.

• Don't clench your fists. Run with your hands relaxed at the ends of your arms.

Your first run

For you starting runners, here's some advice that may seem a little silly: your first run should be a walk. If you think of running as the opposite of standing, walking is in the middle. So start in the middle.

Brisk walking for a few days is the prudent way to start a running program that within three months may have you breezing as much as two to five miles. It depends on how much you want, how old you are, and how good you are at it.

Those early brisk-walking days will help give your muscles the idea that soon you're going to ask more of them than a run down the block. At the same time, you can start to figure out where you'll want to run. If there are other runners in the neighborhood, ask them for a good mile-long course.

See if you can plot a course that ends about a five minute walk from where you live. One thing to remember is that it's as important to cool down after a run as it is to warm up before one.

And the best way to cool down is to walk for five minutes or more after you finish running. Don't just flop on the ground. Walk after you run. It lets your body readjust gradually.

Run, walk, run

Most of you probably won't pay any attention to our prudent advice about starting out with brisk walking. That's okay—as long as you don't hurt yourself. Some people like to live dangerously. Your choice.

Once you start running, don't forget about walking. Remember, nobody expects anything that first day. As a matter of fact, a nice thing about running is that you can do it all on your own. You don't have to please anybody—except yourself. You aren't competing with anyone. Just go your own mild, slow pace, and enjoy yourself.

One good way to start would be to jog slowly for two or three minutes, and then walk briskly for a couple of minutes. Then jog slowly for a few minutes again. Go this walk-run-walk route for twenty to thirty minutes every other day for the first couple of weeks.

If you prefer, measure your running in terms of distance. Start adding miles slowly. Most coaches suggest increasing distance first, then speed.

After a couple of weeks, you'll probably find you are running more and walking less. Just keep it up at the pace you find comfortable. Don't overdo it. You'll find you are running faster and farther from week to week. Let your body tell you how far to go and how fast.

A little faster

Remember, the way you'll improve your cardiovascular fitness is by slowly pushing yourself. Every week or two, you should try to set a little goal for yourself. See if you can make it to the next tree down the path. After a while, you'll be jogging with ease what was impossible a few weeks ago. Then set a more ambitious goal—thirty minutes of continuous running or three miles.

But never get too proud to stop and walk—even if you went farther the last time you were running. You won't improve every time you run. Some days, it will seem like you're running uphill the whole day. Other days, you'll feel like a feather. You'll improve, but you won't be able to notice it every time you run. You'll realize it by looking back over the weeks.

Go at your own pace, and enjoy yourself.

Janeart/Jane Sobel

Keep Running

9

Running should be fun. By that we don't mean it should always be easy. Overcoming difficulties is the fast route to satisfaction, and that's a kind of fun. But on the whole running should never be boring or distasteful. You shouldn't dislike it.

In this chapter we want to show you some ways to avoid the boredom that some runners complain about. You're running alone nearly every day, on perhaps the same route and you know every tree by name. The answer if you're bored: run with a friend.

If none of your friends do, it's not hard to find someone who already runs on your normal route who's just waiting to be asked, "Mind if I run with you?"

If that fails, or even if it doesn't, try running with your mother, or brother or father or sister or aunt. A running companion — friend or family — will motivate you, provide a challenge, and give you someone to talk to while you run (and you should always be able to talk during a run — if you can't, you're running too fast or too far).

If you're still bored, here are some running games:

• *Pass the Olympic Torch:* Decide where the Olympic Games are being held. Choose a city where they have taken place or will in the future and figure out the mileage from there to your home. Divide this distance among members of your family, or a group of your friends and see how long it would take you *as a team* to relay the torch from home to light the next Olympiad.

• *Running around America:* Calculate the distance of nearby cities and see how many you can reach in a week or a month. Race with your running companion across the U. S. from your home to the most distant border or coast and see who's first. You'll probably feel great knowing you've beaten your father in a run from Cleveland to the West Coast without ever having left your neighborhood.

• *Sprint and Wait:* If you run on a track divide it in half (in your head, that is), then sprint half way around and wait while your partner jogs to catch up with you. Then you jog half the track while your partner sprints. This is good "interval training," something we'll talk about in a bit. Even if you don't run on a track, you can still sprint and wait on your normal running route—just take turns in jogging and sprinting for one or two minutes.

• *Breaking World Records:* Look up some old running records—the two-mile in 1900, for example, and see how close you can get to it. You'll be amazed when you look at these old records how standards have risen in this century for both men and women.

Fitness trails

These trails were developed in Europe to promote all-around fitness. Running routes are marked and divided at quarter-mile intervals by "stations" where the runner would find instructions to perform certain exercises—maybe twenty sit-ups or ten push-ups. The idea is to exercise the parts of the body that running doesn't develop, particularly the upper body.

Some American cities now have these trails (often called Parcours) with stations where you're instructed to climb ropes, swing back and forth on rings as well as do the more conventional exercises. If you've got one in your town, you're lucky. If you don't, it's easy, alone or with a running companion, to devise one. Divide up your normal routes into quarter-mile segments and then do a certain number of sit-ups, push-ups or the strengthening exercises we describe in Chapter Seven. It might be more interesting if you include a local playground in your run. Climb the jungle gym or hanging ladder, walk around the edge of the sandbox without losing your balance, and then carry on with your run.

Organized running

Some of you will want to challenge yourselves by running against kids your own age or even against adults in long races. Others of you will find the most exciting challenge

Running Across America

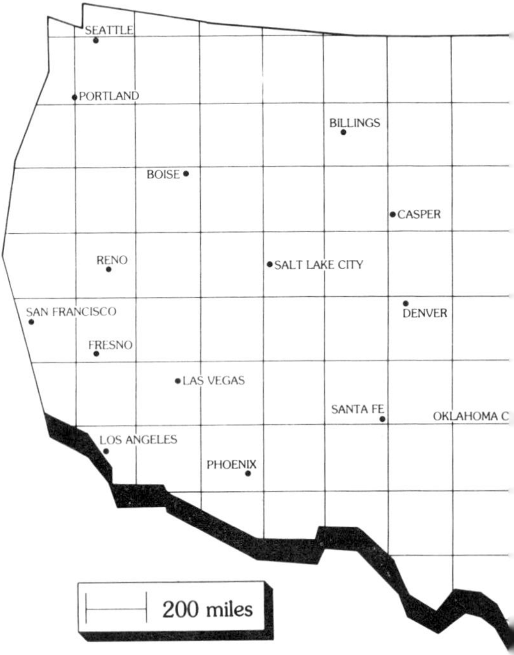

Keep a record of the number of miles you run each week.

See what cities you can reach.
In fifty-two weeks what will be your total mileage?

CONCORD
BOSTON
MINNEAPOLIS
ROCHESTER
BUFFALO
DETROIT
NEW YORK
CHICAGO
CLEVELAND
PHILADELPHIA
DES MOINES
WASHINGTON, D.C.
LINCOLN
INDIANAPOLIS
RICHMOND
NASHVILLE
CHARLOTTE
FORT SMITH
ATLANTA
DALLAS
FORT WORTH
TALLAHASSEE
JACKSONVILLE
NEW ORLEANS
HOUSTON
MIAMI

Total Miles

in running cross-country or in a sport new to the U. S. —orienteering. Here are some points on all these activities and some advice on training if competitive running appeals to you.

• *Age-group Competitions:* If you want to find out how you compare as a runner with others your age, both in your area and throughout the country, get in touch with the local track club or Athletics Congress. They coordinate a nationwide track competition for different age groups from six to eighteen. Competitions are held in all track events, from short sprints to two-mile runs. Write them at Athletics Congress, 3400 W. 86th Street, Indianapolis, Indiana 46268.

• *Cross-country Running:* Up hill, down dale, across streams, under fences, over hurdles—that's cross-country running. It's undoubtedly interesting running and it certainly provides you with good conditioning. As you run on uneven and soft ground and up and down hills, you help make your legs and ankles much stronger. Cross-country running also helps you develop a relaxed running style.

Psychologically, it's also good for you, because as international coach Arthur Lydiard says, "the greatest advantage of cross-country running is that parents cannot follow alongside, urging young runners to run faster and more intensely than they are physically and mentally prepared to do." As Lydiard says, you tend to run at speeds that make you pleasantly tired, rather than exhausted.

There are cross-country meets held throughout the country. For information write Athletics Congress at above address, or check with your local track club.

• *Orienteering:* This variation on cross-country running was developed in Sweden to make fitness more attractive to students. At the beginning of the course you are given a map on which checkpoints are marked. With the aid of a compass you must find your way between all these checkpoints to the finish line. At each checkpoint your map will be marked to show you've been there. It's a sport with all the advantages of cross-country, plus you get to be a whiz with a map and compass. For more information, write: U. S. Orienteering Federation, 505 Stephanie Lane, Manchester, Missouri 63011.

• *Marathons:* You probably know that there are some very young marathoners. Like Kathy Briant, now eleven, who's been running marathons since she was eight, and Paul Masson, ten, who has run the marathon in less than three hours. Before trying to do it, too, you should think seriously about what it would mean to your life and your running. As we said in Chapter Three, doctors still don't know what this kind of hard running and training will do to your body. There are a lot of opinions, but little real evidence. Some experts fear it will damage the growth plates at the end of long bones. Others believe it won't. Some doctors merely think it's silly for children to be guided by adult goals—and 26 miles, 385 yards is certainly an adult goal. Well, depending on how you look at it, others say it's childish.

You must decide for yourself about marathon running—don't let your parents or coaches push you into it. Remember, it will require a dedication in training that will cut you off from a lot of life's other pleasures. And if you're not careful, running will stop being fun. If you do decide to try marathon running then you must get a trainer—preferably a trainer experienced in working with long-distance runners. You can find a trainer through your local Road Runners Club. The track team coach at your school or at a local university might also be a good source.

Training

There are three training methods commonly used today. They all have benefits. None is clearly best. Different runners do well with each method. Your trainer will use one or all of these methods depending on what you're training for, and what has worked best for him or her in the past.

The 1980 Olympic Torch Run from Olympia, Greece to Lake Placid, New York

The route of the Olympic torch bearers originated in Olympia Greece, the site of the original Olympic Games. On January 30, 1980 the torch was carried by a runner to Athens where it was transported aboard U.S. Air Force One to Langley, Virginia. The torch route from Virginia to Lake Placid was completed by 52 runners, one from every state plus the District of Columbia and the host village of Lake Placid.

These torch bearers covered 1,000 miles during a nine day journey across the Eastern seaboard. If you represented your state as an Olympic torch bearer, how long would it take you to run 18 miles?

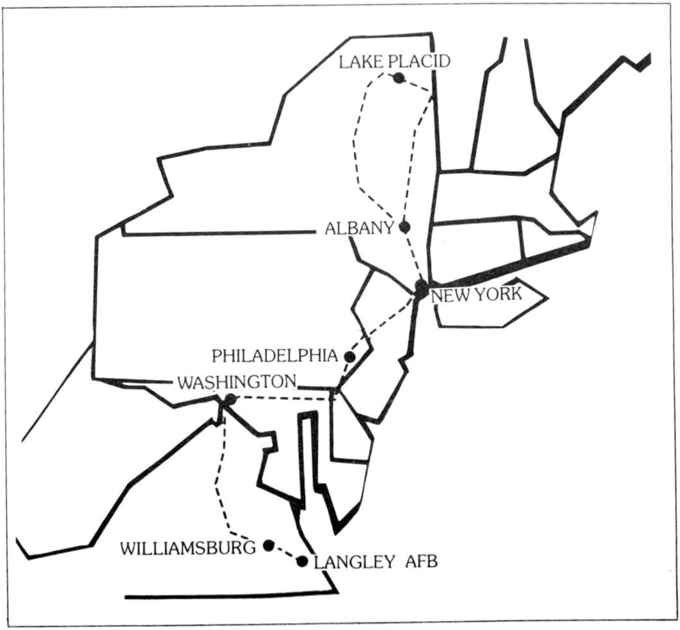

• *Interval Training:* With this method, you run a series of repeat distances with a controlled amount of rest in-between each run. What you do is run quarter miles (or shorter distances) at a speed slower than you plan to race and then rest. Fast interval training also conditions the muscles you're using. Here you run the quarter miles at close to race speed, but rest longer.

• *Repetition Training:* The principle here is to run each quarter mile (if you're training for the mile) at a faster and faster rate, but resting between quarters to allow your heartbeat to return to normal. This gradually pushes up the speed at which you can run a full mile because your muscles and cardiovascular system learn to compensate for breathlessness—or what doctors call "oxygen debt." What made you breathless at first won't after awhile. It will be manageable when you've practiced a bit and adapted to the training.

• *LSD:* Long Slow Distance running has been most successfully used by Arthur Lydiard and Dr. Ernst Van Aaken, both of whom have trained several Olympic running champions. The object is to cover as many miles as possible. You do this by slowing when you're tired, then speeding up as you recover. But you never push yourself to the point of breathlessness, and you don't stop until the predetermined finish point. This method develops endurance and muscular strength and is particularly effective training for long distance events.

If you're just running your own personal race, for your own enjoyment, then use these techniques to vary your workouts. But if you're into serious competition then work on them with your trainer.

Remember, an important rule in running is to have fun. Be guided by it.

Running Clubs

10

Sharing is at once a pleasure and a virtue. So you might have a real good time starting a running club. And it could be an experience you'll look back on for a lifetime.

A running club provides a ready-made pool of friends with whom you can run. But that's only one benefit. Even if you like to run alone, and a lot of people do, it's nice to have friends your age with whom you can share experiences and pass on advice.

A running club can be the information exchange for such nuggets of wisdom as the turf of the mean dog that's just moved into the neighborhood, the site of a chuckhole where runners have tripped, the latest in running-shoe lore, and the best way to avoid blisters.

And a running club can be the best way for you to set up the fun runs and races that will keep the sport an endless source of enjoyment. Write to the magazine, *Runner's World,* for their fun-run information. (World Publications, Box 366, 1400 Stierlin Road, Mountain View, California 94042.)

Electing officers

First off, elect yourself president. Then start looking for other members. It's easiest to become president when you're the only member.

You'll soon find that there are two kinds of members of any club. One kind just likes to belong. The other kind likes to run the club and do the work. A club needs both kinds.

Since you're starting the club, you're probably the kind of person who likes to organize and run things. So find some friends to help you get going.

The first one who agrees can be vice-president. The next secretary, and the one after that treasurer. Keep the title of race director for yourself—in reserve. You can give it up, if necessary, to some new member who wants to be an officer. Or, you might want to select a different race director for each race, making it a title of honor.

For other members who demand titles, you can set up committees. For instance, a member can be chairman of the shoe committee—in charge of keeping up with the latest information on good running shoes. Another can head up the trophy-and-awards committee—in charge of getting ribbons or trophies to winners of races or special achievements (such as most-improved runner).

There might be a publicity committee assigned to getting news of your races and activities, such as fund-raising, on local radio and TV shows and into the newspapers. You might want publicity to tell people you're going to have a race, and then you'll certainly want publicity after the race with the names of the winners.

There can be as many committees as you have ideas and members.

Finding the dollars

Now dues. An effective club has to do things now and then, and they usually cost the club a little money. So figure out what dues you want to charge—but don't overdo it. One way to get a little extra money for your treasury is to ask your parents to be associate members.

Eventually, if your club thrives, you'll get more ambitious and want to organize weekend trips for running, hiking, and camping holidays, or you may want to set up races with clubs in other towns. One way to make money is to sell T-shirts with the club name on them. Car washes and bake sales are also good ways to raise some funds.

So you may have to try for funds outside the family. If you live in a small town or city, try the mayor's office. City recreational authorities sometimes set money aside just for this kind of thing. Get one of the associate members to try the governor's office in your state capital. There's probably a state fitness commission that can help.

And road runners

There may be a Road Runner's Club for adults in your city, and your club may want to affiliate with it. The Road Runners can certainly offer you advice. Road Runners

Club of America has a member-at-large category. Or, perhaps your club can *become* the Road Runners Club for your community.

The New York Road Runners sponsor a national age-group cross-country competition every November in New York City's Van Cortlandt Park with more than 3,000 youngsters your age competing from many states. It was one of the first big races for today's middle-distance star, Jan Merrill.

If you're interested, write Barry Geisler, Chairman, National Age Group Cross-Country Championship, 2676 Morris Avenue, Bronx, New York 10468.

Club runs

The main purpose of the club is up to you. Maybe you just want it as a place to exchange information about running. But for most clubs, running together three or four times a week is the main reason for getting organized.

Your club can keep records for its members—if the members want—on how often they run, how far, how fast, and their general progress.

Your club can negotiate with school authorities about using school facilities. You might want to use the school as a headquarters for races because it has bathrooms and drinking fountains.

Your club can set up weekend family races, giving the associate members a chance to show their stuff. Families can race as teams against other families.

Or every other week your club can sponsor a family or community fun jog—without any competition. It's not necessary to race all the time. Sometimes it's nice when everybody just gets together and has a good run.

Probably most important, however, is that your club be both active and fun. Don't take the club too seriously. Don't make a lot of unnecessary rules. The best clubs have the fewest regulations and the most laughs.

Index